DOGHOUSE

by the same author

Fred in Situ
The Loose Screw
Mud in His Eye
Dead Game
The Reward Game
The Revenge Game
Fair Game
The Game
Cousin Once Removed
Sauce for the Pigeon
Pursuit of Arms
Silver City Scandal
The Executor
The Worried Widow
Adverse Report
Stray Shot
Dog in the Dark
A Brace of Skeet
Whose Dog Are You?
Let Us Prey
Home to Roost
In Camera

DOGHOUSE

Gerald Hammond

St. Martin's Press
New York

 For information, address St. Martin's Press, 175 Fifth Avenue, New York, N.Y. 10010.

Library of Congress Cataloging-in-Publication Data

Hammond, Gerald
Doghouse / Gerald Hammond.
p. cm.
ISBN 0-312-07733-5
I. Title.
PR6058.A55456D64 1992
823'.914—dc20 92-4523
CIP

First published in Great Britain by Macmillan London Limited.

First U.S. Edition: August 1992
10 9 8 7 6 5 4 3 2 1

DOGHOUSE

One

Beth, usually the most deferential and retiring of company, had been laying down the law for some minutes without visibly drawing breath. She was now winding up to her peroration. 'Is it a turd? Is it a brain?' she demanded rhetorically, pointing an accusing finger at me. 'No. It's Blooperman! You,' she added firmly, 'are an idiot.'

Isobel Kitts, my only other partner, raised her eyebrows but said nothing. Isobel took a pride in never watching television and she had probably never heard of Superman. Secretly, I had thought Beth's multiple pun quite witty, although I would never have admitted it. Isobel was merely puzzled.

Beth was my kennelmaid. I could, I suppose, have sacked her from that post on the spot. But she was by then also my fiancée and the third partner in the business and I had no desire to displace her from any one of those three positions. She was the one bright spot in a rather grisly world and she did nearly all of the hard work for a salary which, while never generous, seemed to have lapsed altogether with the change to her status. So I kept a check on my tongue, which sometimes gets beyond my control and develops a cutting edge.

'I know it,' I said mildly. I had pulled up a chair and was huddled against the kitchen boiler, letting the delicious warmth of it soothe away the chill.

Isobel looked up again from the accounts which she had spread over the kitchen table and scowled at me over her unsuitably pink-framed spectacles. 'So you bloody well should, John,' she said. 'If you have to go off your rocker, do it where we can keep an eye on you.'

Isobel was a strong-minded woman and as her age must almost have equalled Beth's and mine added together – although she would never have forgiven either of us had we dared to remind her of the fact – she was rather a mother figure in the business. She lived a couple of miles away with Henry, her elderly husband; but the pair seemed to spend far more time at Three Oaks Kennels than they did at their home.

There was a very small element of justice in their complaints. I had awoken that morning, suddenly and completely and with a sense of wellbeing such as I had not known since my days in the army. Some sort of combined celebration and test seemed to be called for. I had thought of waking Beth for an essay at lovemaking – I omitted to mention that she was also my mistress – but a protracted illness had left my performance in that regard less than reliable. A grumpy word would have guaranteed failure, upsetting Beth, humiliating me and spoiling what was shaping up to be one of the better days.

Instead, I had slipped quietly out of bed, dressed in the dark and left a note of explanation on the kitchen table. A drive of half an hour and a five minute walk had brought me to a well-remembered reed-bank on the River Tay, and I had been in place in time to hear the geese talking before they began to take off on their dawn flight to the feeding grounds. The sight and sound of the skeins coming off the water in the light of a scarlet dawn would have been reward enough. It was the scene which I had missed most of all during my illness.

My return home was greeted by two enraged ladies loudly competing with each other to list the greater number of my follies.

Although the London School of Tropical Medicine had pronounced my blood clear at last of the parasite which had been enfeebling me for years, and although even the damage to my organs was slowly reversing, I might have remembered that I was still seriously underweight. The chill of a winter's dawn seemed to have penetrated deeper than my bones and into my very soul, and my two guardians were unanimous in prophesying horrid relapses in my state of health.

But even that piece of idiocy took second place, slightly ahead of the ruination of my clothes by Tay mud and on a par with the rashness of venturing onto a tidal foreshore without telling anybody where I was going so that, at the very least, they could have instituted a search for my body if I had been swept away. The greatest sin of all had been to take Samson with me.

On my return, still high on the euphoria of a perfect outing, I had exhibited my prize of a handsome greylag goose. I should have left it at that but, through chattering teeth, I had rashly gone on to praise Samson, who had taken the plunge into icy water and pursued the stricken goose out of sight, swept upstream on the flood tide, to struggle back an hour later along the shore with the weight of the now dead goose balanced high in his jaws.

At that point my health had been relegated from

first concern to comparative insignificance. If I had to jeopardise my recovery, they asked, was it also necessary to risk Samson?

'He's the best dog we've got in water,' I pointed out.

'He is also the prop and mainstay of the business,' Isobel retorted.

If that was an exaggeration, there was at least a degree of truth in it. I had been invalided out of the army with no assets except a modest pension, two well-pedigreed springer spaniel bitches and a knack of training dogs. After several years of occasionally successful competition in field trials (which had enhanced the selling price of litters considerably) I had been coaxed into setting up a more professional breeding and training kennels for springer spaniels, with Isobel as partner. Beth had come as a later but valuable addition.

Abercraig Samson was our prime stud dog. His elevation to the title of Field Trials Champion had contributed substantially to our modest success. Our practice of offering generous discounts to field trials competitors whom we regarded as skilled trainers and handlers had proved a wise investment. His progeny were figuring regularly in lists of awards and creating a steady demand for puppies and trained dogs and for his services at stud.

'He's getting on in years,' Isobel finished. 'You've probably killed him.'

This was so patently false that I could ignore it. Samson, towelled into a fluffy ball, was sprawled against the stove at my feet, steaming gently and obviously very pleased with himself. It does wonders for a field trials dog to be reminded occasionally that there is a real and engrossing world outside of the tight discipline of competitions and picking-up.

'If he gets crippled with rheumatism, he'll be too stiff to mount a bitch,' Beth added.

This also was false. Samson was the randiest dog in the business and with an extraordinary power over the opposite sex. During my long convalescence I had often envied him. His mongrel by-blows could be recognised for several miles around. We tried to keep him in confinement, more because of his value than for the sake of the local bitch-owners, but Samson could detect a bitch in season at a thousand yards despite all the Amplex and Antimate in the world, and when he had caught the scent it would have taken a Chubb safe to restrain him. He had once sired a litter while confined in the boot of a small car with a bitch who was only beginning to come into season. I strongly suspected that at least part of his hour adrift had been spent in serving the bitches of Balmerino or even Inchture.

'All *right*,' I said. Even to myself, I sounded petulant. 'So I went mad for a morning. It may never happen again. But just for once, I wanted to do something I wanted to do.'

Beth looked at me sharply. Garbled sentences had been a symptom which had preceded the occasional blackout during the worst of my illness. Then she decided that I was trying to say something. 'Yes, but what?' she asked.

'What I mean is that for years now – literally years – I've been leading a sensible life, watching my diet, wrapping up warmly, subjecting myself to medical indignities and never doing a damn thing just for the hell of it in case it gave me a setback. Isobel does the handling in competition— '

'You're welcome to take it over again,' Isobel said.

That stopped me with a jerk. We had most of an

intensive winter's programme of competition ahead of us, because the buyer in search of a pup or a trained dog looks for a winning strain before he parts with his gold. This, after all, is his only guarantee of sound, working stock with innate ability. Isobel had taken over the handling because my health had not been up to the job. She had continued because she was temperamentally better suited to it. She had the knack of staying calm and thinking her way out of a crisis when I might have been shouting and whistling my way towards relegation.

'It's not that,' I said. 'You two do all the real work. Mostly, I just do the training. It's like being a schoolmaster, eternally handing down the same old lessons and correcting the same old faults.'

'Without your training,' Isobel said, 'we'd never win a prize. We'd be lucky to sell a pup for a price which would cover our costs.'

'And besides,' Beth said unhappily, 'you love it. You know you do.' She was trying hard to understand. There were real tears in her brown eyes.

'All right, so I do, usually. But, even accepting that as a fact, don't you think that you could get fed up of eating strawberries and ice cream to the music of Mozart, if you had to do it day in and day out?' Beth nodded uncertainly. 'Just for once I woke up feeling on top of the world. I wanted to go out with a dog and do something real, the sort of thing the dog's meant for, instead of going on for ever teaching him the tricks of his future trade. I wanted . . . ' I paused and tried to order my jumbled thoughts. 'I wanted to do something, anything, which wouldn't bore me out of my skull. I know that sounds bad and it isn't how I feel all the time, but it's how I felt this morning. Can't you understand? I think I've got it out of my system now,' I finished.

Beth and Isobel regarded me in silence. It was doubtful whether they did understand. A woman often copes with monotony better than a man; and she has no instinct to gather meat.

'You need a holiday,' Isobel said. It was her panacea, but not always a practicable one.

'At the end of the season— ' I began.

'That's nearly three months away. We'll have to see what we can arrange.'

Beth and Isobel made eye contact. I knew that they were already mutely conspiring to arrange my life for me, and that I would be helpless under the weight of so much cloying femininity.

'I must go,' Beth said suddenly. 'Dogs don't look after themselves. And pups have to be fed.'

'I'll give you a hand,' I said.

Beth shook her head so that her dark hair danced. 'Definitely not,' she said. 'I'm going to run you a hot bath and you can go back to bed for the rest of the morning.'

'While I put the little beggars through their paces,' Isobel said. She began to gather up her papers.

'You'll feel better by lunchtime,' Beth said firmly. It was an order.

I wanted to rebel and say that no, I bloody well wouldn't feel better by lunchtime if I didn't want to. But my lost sleep was beginning to overtake me. I followed her upstairs like a well-trained pup.

The fact that Beth and Isobel were, in principle, absolutely right would only have added to my irritation – if I had been awake to think about it. But I fell into a bottomless pool of sleep for two full hours. I plunged so deep that even memory seemed to be wiped clean. When Beth awoke me with a mug of soup at lunch-time, I surfaced in a room which looked familiar and yet strange. I had to think hard for a while to orient myself and remember that Beth, when she moved in with me, had imported some touches of colour which changed the room just as her own colour had changed my life. It was still a bare room, oddly shaped by being tucked into the roof with a dormer for its window, and its redecoration was somewhere near the tail-end of our list of priorities, but a new pair of curtains, some ornaments and a collage of flower pictures on the wardrobe doors had both humanised it and made it into alien territory.

As she had predicted, I felt better. I was both amused and irked to admit that she could order my mood to change.

While I sipped and waited for the soup to cool, Beth perched on the side of the bed and stared at me solemnly, as though I had suddenly grown another head. She was in her middle to late twenties but she still looked about fifteen. Partly it was the long legged, small busted, coltish build of her, but she also had the small nose, large eyes and lovely complexion of the pubescent girl. She kept a copy of her birth certificate in her handbag alongside her driving licence, for the benefit of disbelieving policemen and barmen.

'Your old goose is hanging in the feed store,' she said. 'Remind me in a few days and I'll pluck and dress it and pop it into the freezer. You're not just bored with me, are you?' she asked without any change of tone. 'Because, if you are, I'll go away.'

I put out my spare hand and she took it shyly. 'Of course not,' I said. 'I love you to bits. If you went away, I'd kill myself.'

'Really?' She seemed uncertain whether to be pleased at the compliment or horrified at the idea.

'Truly,' I said. 'But suddenly this morning I felt as if I'd done nothing for years except cosset my health and be a passenger in my own business. And physically I had all my energy back, with compound interest. Try to imagine what it was like, to wake up suddenly with an unfamiliar feeling and then to realise that it was the sensation of feeling fit again. Can you?'

Beth wrinkled her brow for a moment and then shook her head.

'I wanted to do something mildly adventurous for a change. It's the wrong time of year for hang-gliding and I couldn't spare the time to explore the Amazon, so I went wildfowling. And, what's more, I enjoyed it and I feel better for it. Big deal!'

Beth hesitated, uncertain which of my arguments to demolish first. 'You aren't a passenger,' she said at last. 'You mustn't think like that. Isobel does the handling because she doesn't get as het up as you do. You do most of the training because you have the patience and you seem to know how a dog's mind works. And all I do is shovel food into one end of them and clean up what comes out of the other.'

'And balance their diets and bathe and brush them and nurse them when they're ill, search them for ticks, weed the garden, do the housework and look after me like a mother hen. And chauffeur Isobel to and from the trials,' I added. Isobel was usually a sober and worthy citizen but she had a habit of celebrating a good result, sometimes far beyond the limits set by the breathalyser.

'I'll do less, if that's what you want.'

'The place would grind to a halt.'

'Don't be silly,' Beth said, both gratified and reassured. 'You're just stale. You need a break.'

I decided to give up. Arguing with women can be as profitless as trying to pump up a burst tyre. Anyway, she was probably right. 'If you say so,' I said.

'I've been talking with Isobel – and don't look up at the ceiling in that fed-up way,' she added sternly. 'Isobel says that she and Henry could look after the place for a few days if we wanted to go away this weekend. There aren't any trials on.'

'I ought to be sharpening Gargany up for the Novice Stake the weekend after,' I said weakly. I had put down strong roots at Three Oaks but, all the same, the prospect of a period of escape, and of having Beth to myself without the chaperonage of a pack of spaniels, was attractive. 'Where would we go?'

Beth stopped meeting my eye. 'I thought that we might go and collect my dog,' she said in a small voice.

I blinked at her. Something seemed to have slipped out of gear. 'What dog?'

'Yes. I only heard yesterday. I was waiting for a good chance to tell you.' Which was a less than satisfactory answer. I drank my soup and waited for her to go on.

'You remember about my uncle?'

'The one who was killed in an accident? You went to his funeral the other week?'

'I never had more than the one uncle. And you know my cousin, Edgar?'

'Vaguely,' I said. I had bumped into Edgar Lawrence at occasional gundog trials – a thin and rather intense man who worked near Glasgow and who bred and trained Labradors in his spare time in a haphazard, semi-professional way. He had talent and had had some successes, but there seemed to be something in his temperament which would always prevent him from reaching the top. 'Is he the son?'

'Edgar's the son of my mother's sister,' she explained. 'Uncle George and Hattie never had any children. You'd have liked my uncle. He was a wildlife artist living at Tarbet – the one on Loch Lomond,' she explained carefully, 'not Tarbert, Loch Fyne, or any of the others.'

She was beginning to wake echoes in my mind. 'Not George Muir?' I asked.

'Yes.'

'I never knew he was your uncle,' I said. 'I saw that he was killed in an accident, but you never said much about him and I never connected the two. I know his work. His wildlife paintings were good. I don't know a hell of a lot about art, but he seemed to be able to catch the attitude of a bird or an animal just the way I've seen it in the wild. He did dogs as well – or even better. I was hoping to get him to do a portrait of Samson, one of these days, if we got rich while the old chap – Samson, I mean – was still on the go.'

'Uncle George left me a picture,' Beth said.

This sounded more and more interesting. An original by George Muir was just what the sitting room needed. 'What of?' I asked.

'I'm to choose from the canvases in his studio. But he also left me a dog.'

I was more interested in the painting, but decided to follow up the dog. 'All right,' I said, 'tell me about the dog,' and thereby unleashed another of Beth's rare bouts of loquaciousness.

'Uncle George did a lot of wildfowling. In recent

years, because he was beginning to get on, he didn't take it so seriously. I mean, he didn't go plowtering a mile out through the mud any more. But he still got a lot of satisfaction, and the inspiration for most of his paintings, out of his trips to the foreshore. That's why I said that you'd have liked him. His old dog, Mona, was getting very stiff and rheumaticky after a life spent in and out of freezing water. Now do you understand why I was so concerned about Samson?' she asked.

'I don't think that once will have done him any harm,' I said. 'Go on.'

'Uncle George bought a Labrador puppy from Edgar about a year ago and paid him in advance to train it. Well, sort of bought it. He liked one of Edgar's bitches, so he paid the stud fee for a really good sire in return for the first choice of a pup. He could have trained it himself – a wildfowler's dog doesn't have to be anything marvellous, does it? – but instead he paid Edgar a fee to train it. I think that he was doing Edgar a favour. Edgar's usually short of money. Clients don't like his manner.

'My uncle left everything to Hattie, of course, except for a few small bequests. But he knew that I was involved with dogs, while Hattie hardly knows a dog from a dodo. I mean, she can feed them and she pats them if they're there and takes them for walks if she happens to feel like walking. She'll give Mona a good enough home for the rest of her life and they'll get along all right, but she has no real feeling for them. And I was always his favourite. So he left the puppy to me. He's called Jason after a favourite dog Uncle George had years ago.'

Something was nagging at a corner of my mind.

'If you were at the funeral, how is it that you only heard yesterday?' I asked.

'Hattie wasn't at the funeral. Uncle George's death gave her such a shock that she was sent to hospital. I only got her letter yesterday morning, enclosing the pedigree.'

'Has Isobel checked it?' I asked. Isobel maintained an astonishing mass of information about gundog blood-lines.

Beth nodded. 'Isobel says that there's no hip dysplasia in the pedigree and no progressive retinal atrophy for ten generations back. And there are both Show Champions and Field Trials Champions in the pedigree.'

'I wouldn't set too much store by that,' I said. 'When you mix show and working dogs, you often get the worst of each.'

'Not so often with Labs,' she said quickly.

'Maybe not.' I sighed. This was going to be difficult. 'But you know that we agreed not to have personal dogs around the place. Dogs are our business and we have to be unsentimental about them.'

She laughed at me. 'Look who's talking,' she said. 'Whenever we sell a pup you carry on as though the buyer was asking for the hand of your daughter.'

'Our daughter,' I said. 'That makes a difference.'

'Our daughter,' she repeated, wide-eyed. 'Golly! I can just see you asking our daughter's boyfriend whether he's got adequate kennel space and an enclosed run and whether he knows about worming. Don't laugh, I mean it. Anyway – be fair, John – I didn't go out to look for a dog. He was left to me. He sort of happened. And I thought that if you're going to go after ducks and geese in rotten weather it would be better if you had a dog for the purpose which wasn't one of our breeding stock. And a Labrador would be better than a spaniel for wildfowling anyway. They sit still for longer.'

'There's some sense in that,' I said, 'but not a lot.' It seemed a good moment to begin negotiating from a position of strength. 'If you and Isobel are going to kick up hell every time I go off in pursuit of our Christmas dinner— '

She knew exactly what I was up to, of course. Beth's youthful appearance and sometimes inconsequential remarks often fooled me into thinking of her and even treating her as a dimwit. But she had a keen mind and a sort of animal cunning. 'You're probably right,' she said. 'I was going to suggest that we went to Hattie for the weekend. She suggested it herself. She's back on her feet now and she sounds lonely. Then we could have picked out my picture and taken a run to visit Edgar. You could have told me whether Jason looked like being worth his keep. But we can skip it if you like. We'll go to that hotel near Kelso instead.'

The message was clear. No dog, no painting.

'All right,' I said. 'We'll do it your way. I could take a gun and see whether the geese are still coming in at Crinan.'

My message was equally clear. No wildfowling, no dog.

She was ready for me. 'I don't think there'd be time. You always say that it's immoral to go shooting without a good dog because of the danger of leaving wounded birds behind – that's part of your sales patter when the purchaser jibs at paying our prices. Mona's too old and stiff. Even if we brought Jason away with us, you couldn't get back and reach Crinan in time for the evening flight. And there's no shooting on a Sunday.'

'I could take Samson,' I said.

'Definitely not,' she retorted. Negotiations were at an end and compromises had been reached which were acceptable to both parties. I was not going to Crinan. On the other hand, I could still reject Jason. The door was open for future wildfowling forays provided that I was accompanied by Jason and not Samson.

Beth decided to return to a more important subject. 'You're sure that what was bothering you was just a general discontent left over from the boring time you had while you were ill? You're not tired of Three Oaks and the business? And me?'

There is only one satisfactory answer to that sort of question. I pulled her closer and reassured her with little kisses. One minute later I had her under the covers with me. Coaxing her out of her jeans and sweater under the duvet made it all seem novel and exciting again.

Her tousled head popped out suddenly. 'Wait,' she said breathlessly. 'Not now. Save it. I've got the dogs' main meals to prepare.'

'I've already done them,' said Isobel's voice from the landing. We heard her go into the bathroom. The toilet was flushed.

So also was Beth. 'She heard us!'

Isobel's feet descended the stairs with deliberate loudness.

'Who cares?' I said. 'We didn't tell her anything she didn't know before.'

When it came, it was tender and perfect. I only just stopped myself from making some comparison with the days before my illness. But I had not known Beth in those days.

Two

We were late getting away from Three Oaks on the Friday afternoon. For this we shared the blame. One of the pups in training, which had previously regarded the whole question of fetching and carrying as a waste of his valuable time, had suddenly decided that retrieving was his mission in life and it was important to impress the lesson before he forgot it again. And Beth was so determined to leave the house and kennels spick and span for Isobel and Henry that she was dusting cobwebs off the wire mesh of the runs and had to be dissuaded from applying metal polish.

We made a pact to be more sensible in the future, took one last walk round together just to be sure that our livestock was comfortable, tick-free and neither gaining nor losing weight, and got on the road just as the sun dipped behind the low hills of Fife. Isobel waved us off, no doubt with a sigh of relief.

We had put in a hard day and my tiredness must have shown. Beth drove the rather weary old estate car which served both as our personal and canine transporter. She was a good driver, so good that I laid my head back and dozed for part of the way. We went by way of Perth and Crieff and Lochearnhead – a scenic route by daylight, but now a black void spewing sudden, blinding lights of onrushing traffic. Between lights, the outlines of the hills against moonlit clouds grew ever taller as we travelled to the west. We had passed Crianlarich and were heading down Glen Falloch towards Loch Lomondside before the traffic died and Beth could spare attention for chatter. It seemed a good time, before we set eyes on Jason and Beth became too enamoured of him, to make sure that we both understood our tacit agreement.

'I'd have thought there were more than enough dogs in your life already,' I said into the darkness. 'Why do you want to take on another?'

'Uncle George wanted me to have him.'

'That doesn't mean that you have to keep him,' I pointed out. 'If his pedigree's so good, you could always sell him. Uncle George wouldn't know.'

'I'd know. I'd feel that I'd let him down. And I want you to have a proper retriever when you go wildfowling.'

'I do appreciate the kind thought, but if you're going to get in a tizzy every time I go to the foreshore— '

'If I could be sure that you were all right, I wouldn't mind so much,' she said. 'You need new waders and some thermal undies. Perhaps we could shop in Glasgow tomorrow.' She fell silent while she screwed her eyes against the glare and squeezed past an oncoming tanker. 'Perhaps I'd be less worried if I came with you— '

I tried to visualise Beth sitting still and quietly in hiding through a freezing dawn, and failed. 'Isobel would get restive if we both started skiving off,' I said.

Beth drove in silence for another mile. 'If you really want to know— ' she said suddenly. Then she fell silent again.

'I do want to know,' I said.

It came out with a rush. 'You've more or less said it yourself a dozen times. And yet you only look at it from your own selfish viewpoint. You complain and feel hard done by and left out of things. Well, you don't have a monopoly of getting fed-up.'

'Hold on,' I said. 'What's this leading up to?'

'To this. You and Isobel get all the fun and I'm just the food-fetcher and shit-shoveller. I help with the training when you're not available or an extra pair of hands is needed, but when it comes to the things which make or break the business I'm out in the cold. Well, all right, somebody has to do it and I don't mind, it's what I came for in the first place. But, just once in a while, I'd like to pull my weight. You've heard of what they call job satisfaction?'

I knew exactly what she meant and I felt a sudden pang of sympathy. 'If you want, we could let you try handling one of the young spaniels in a Puppy Stake,' I said.

Beth snorted, took a bend too fast and had to jerk the wheel. She slowed right down. 'Isobel's the tops,' she said, 'and you know it. I'd feel terrible if I spoiled our record. Anyway, I'm not up to working spaniels in a field trial, not to winning standard. But I always go along with Isobel to the trials, just to give her moral support and a drive home, and some clubs run spaniels and retrievers on the same day. I could enter with Jason in a Retriever Trial without making a total muck-up of it – the worst thing that can happen with a retriever is getting its eye wiped – and it wouldn't harm the business if I came last or got put out. Or don't you think I could do it?'

Consciously or unconsciously, she had found an argument which was bound to appeal to me. To the dedicated spaniel man the work of a mere retriever – walking steadily to heel until there is downed quarry to fetch – seems to be straight out of the kindergarten. As long as the dog doesn't chase a hare or eat the retrieve, its handler can hold up his or her head. A spaniel (which is required to perform the same duties, but also to quest and flush its quarry at some distance from the handler while remaining under perfect control and steadfast against temptation) presents a whole host of additional problems.

'You could do it,' I said. 'But could you do it while still giving the other dogs your full attention?'

'If you ever think I'm neglecting my job,' Beth said bravely, 'you can get rid of him for me. I'll give you that in writing. And I'll pay for his food if that's bothering you.'

In the face of such determination I could only give ground. 'No need for that. We'd better take a look at him,' I said cautiously. 'Your cousin may have ruined him already.'

Beth said nothing, but her driving had regained its usual high standard so I knew that a load had come off her mind.

A meal was already waiting for us and our hostess was hopping with impatience. It had taken us some time to find the house, which was perched on a hillside high above the loch and approached by a succession of minor roads. Occasional lights pinpointed a sprinkling of other dwellings. Beth had visited her uncle several times during his lifetime, but only as a passenger. More than once she was sure that she recognised a road, but the darkness defeated her and each time she was wrong.

Harriet Muir, Beth's aunt by marriage, had evidently been expecting us for some time. Like any good hostess, she wanted to serve the meal before it dehydrated. She brushed aside my conventional words of condolence and gave us a few seconds to wash and examine our (separate) rooms before she had us seated at table in a neat but old-fashioned dining room. The house was a rambling old place. Many owners had left eccentric imprints on it, but if anything had ever been shoddy or out of key it had been remedied. It was a comfortable home, kept up unpretentiously but to a high standard of cleanliness and polish. A faint odour of pipe tobacco still lingered. The meal was conventional Scottish fare, unelaborate but deliciously prepared. The glasses on the table were accompanied by an uncompromising jug of water. I wondered whether this had been a teetotal household but decided that to ask the question would be to suggest criticism.

Hattie – as she asked us both to call her – was a brusque lady in her forties. Her blue-black hair should have been greying, but I detected the unnatural blackness of a famous colour restorer. She was tall, almost stately. She had a soft, West Highland accent quite out of keeping with an authoritative manner.

'You found the place at last,' she observed as we ate.

'At last,' Beth agreed. 'I thought I remembered the way but I didn't. When you're being driven, you see more of the scenery but less of the route.'

'You should have stopped and asked.'

'We did. Three men who were strangers here themselves, one woman with a bad stammer who'd never heard of the place and a drunk who insisted on drawing a map on the back of an envelope.' Beth laughed suddenly. 'We nearly didn't believe him, but he turned out to be absolutely right.'

Hattie nodded slowly. 'That would be Grant Nolan?' she said.

I had slipped the envelope into my pocket rather than drop it in the car. I took it out and looked at the name of the original addressee. 'That's right,' I said. 'How did you know?'

'It would have to be,' she said. 'He's my gardener and odd-job man. And he's the only one of the heavy drinkers around here who would know the way. George could enjoy a dram of an evening, but he only had contempt for boozers. That wasn't among his vices.' She glanced at Beth's hand and her eyes came back to me. 'Beth told me on the phone that you're engaged. I wished her every happiness and I'll wish you the same. When do you plan to tie the knot?'

Beth and I were getting along so comfortably that we had hardly bothered to discuss dates. I was uncertain how to answer. Some West Highlanders are fanatically moral, others believe in marrying just in time to legitimise the first baby. Beth stepped into the moment of silence.

'We're in no hurry,' she said. 'We've been more concerned about John's health.'

'The war wound,' Hattie said, nodding.

Beth, who knew how that remark would irritate me, explained hastily. The longstanding illness which had cut short my army career had resulted from the bite of a leech infected with a rare tropical bug; but rumour in the gundog fraternity, and locally in Fife, persisted in crediting me with having been wounded in the Falklands War.

'He could do with some flesh on his bones,' Hattie said. She made to fill my plate again, but I resisted firmly. I had surprised myself by eating all of a generous first portion.

'He's definitely on the mend now,' Beth said. 'If we have time tomorrow, we thought that we might run into Glasgow and choose a ring.' She gave me a look which warned me not to express surprise. She was indulging Hattie's preconceptions.

Discussion of my health between others always made me feel peculiarly mortal, as though I were in my coffin and they were speaking of whatever had carried me off. (As long as my health remained my own business, I could ignore it or succumb to self-pity according to my mood.) And the choosing of an engagement ring was among the many subjects of my procrastination, because I was torn between competing desires – to give Beth the very best and yet to plough back every penny of my earnings into the house and business.

To turn the subject I said, 'But you've not been well yourself. Beth said that she missed you on the day of the funeral.'

'Doctors!' Hattie said. 'They'll have you walking around on a broken leg and then send you to bed to get over an upset. It was a shock, mind, and I dare say that I was the better for the rest. The fright that I got, I thought that my heart would stop and that I'd be laid to rest beside poor George.'

'You must miss him terribly,' Beth said.

'I'll miss having him around,' Hattie admitted. 'Not that he was much company, always in the studio or away out in the car and painting like a mad thing, or shooting, or with his nose buried in a book. But when he'd finished a picture and he wasn't fishing or away after the geese, then he was a fine husband. And a good provider, I'll say that for him.'

I hoped that Beth would be able to say as much for me when I was gone.

While Hattie rattled on she had been serving up a trifle with cream, giving me no chance to say that I was already full. When I sampled it I found that I still had a little appetite left. Between mouthfuls, I asked, 'What exactly did happen? If you're ready to talk about it . . . When I saw the report of George Muir's death in the paper I didn't realise that he was Beth's uncle, so I only glanced at the heading. And Beth said no more than that he was killed in an accident.'

'That was almost all I knew,' Beth said. 'There seemed to be hundreds of people at the funeral, but every one of them shied away from the subject. They only wanted to talk about what a loss he was to the world of art. But don't talk about it, Hattie, if it still upsets you.'

Hattie put her elbows on the table and looked down between her hands. 'I can talk about it now,' she said quietly. 'At first, I couldn't even think about it but now . . . it's time that I came to terms with it. I'll tell you the way it was.

'George always loaded his own cartridges. Not the ordinary ones – he said that he could buy them as cheaply as he could load them. But he said that the big cartridges for the geese were overpriced. He didn't have one of the new machines, he said that for all the cartridges he fired it'd take fifty years to pay for itself.'

'True,' I said. The foreshore wildfowler, when his luck is out, can go through a season on a dozen cartridges.

'George had an old set of hand tools which he'd bought in a junk shop many years ago. He kept them at the work-bench in his studio. The evening it happened, he was planning to go out with his gun first thing in the morning. He left me in the living room and went through to finish reloading a few more cartridges, just in case the pinkfeet were still using the flight-line he had been watching a few days before, so he said.

'Only a moment later, there was a terrible bang. The house shook and everything in it seemed to rattle and there was a smell of smoke. I ran through. George was on the floor beside his work-bench.' She looked up at us suddenly. 'He was moving. At first, I thought that he might not be badly hurt. But then I saw what was left of his head and there was no doubt in my mind that he was dead or as good as. No man could have lived with so much damage to his head. It was just the nerves still making him move. I think that that was the worst thing about it, him still moving like that although I knew that he had to be dead . . . '

If it had not been self-evident that the mental picture would be distressing to Hattie, her face would have told us. Unable to think of a major change of subject I tried a minor one. 'Did they ever discover how it happened?' I asked.

Hattie's face calmed. 'The police decided that it had been a simple accident. He was a smoker, you see.'

'I expect that they were right,' I said gruffly. I tried and failed to think how to give the conversation another twist.

'Aye.' She looked out of the window into darkness for a few seconds. 'I haven't brought myself to go into the place since that moment,' Hattie said. She seemed ashamed to admit to such a weakness. 'But he was a canny man. He never smoked when he was loading. He aye liked a pipe after his tea, but that evening he'd sat and smoked it in the living room, keeping me company. Only when he'd finished and knocked it out did he go through.'

'And the explosion came just a few seconds later?' Beth asked. 'Could a spark have been clinging to his clothes?'

'It's possible,' Hattie said. 'I used to say I was going to buy him only clothes patterned with little brown spots, so that the burns wouldn't show. But he was aye the first to notice the smell of cloth burning.' She shrugged. 'Likely that's what happened. I can't see it, myself, but it's as difficult to think of any other way. God knows I've tried, though I don't know about these things.' She paused and seemed to give herself a mental shake. When she spoke again, she was back to her brisk and forceful self. 'I don't suppose we'll ever know for sure. Come away through to the living room while I put the kettle on. You'll take a dram?' she asked me. 'George liked a glass after his tea, with his pipe.'

The living room epitomised the house – comfortable, faded, but the furnishings had been the best in their day and were probably worth real money by now, as much even as the three George Muir paintings which hung on the walls. These were plain landscapes without the wildlife with which he had made his name. I guessed that the conventional colours of the room were the choice of Hattie rather than of the artist. A photograph of George Muir stood in a silver frame on the mantel – a man in his late fifties, still slim and upright, with a military moustache. He had an avuncular look but, unless the gleam in his eye was a trick of the photographer's lights, he had had more than a touch of the devil in him. A Labrador with grizzled jowls, dozing in front of the fireplace, spared us no more than a disinterested glance.

Hattie fetched a nearly full Glenfiddich bottle out of a wall cupboard and I accepted a small glass topped up with water. The late Uncle George's habits still prevailed and, while some might have considered them eccentric, my still delicate stomach preferred to receive its occasional helpings of spirits on top of a meal rather than before it.

'While I'm in the kitchen,' Hattie said, 'you may like to go through and choose yourselves one of George's pictures, the way his will said. I doubt there's not many of them are undamaged.'

The word 'doubt', in the Scots language, can mean the very reverse of its English meaning. I puzzled my way through the multiplicity of negatives. 'Don't you want to pick any of the undamaged ones for yourself?' I asked.

'Bless you, I'll not fash myself,' Hattie said, almost cheerfully. 'George's will said that Beth was to get first pick and Edgar next. Edgar's been at me already, wanting to take one for himself, but I said no, he could just wait his turn. These three were my favourites and they're left to me. They'll do.' She nodded to each of the three paintings on the walls, greeting old friends. The places rather than the paintings had memories for her.

'I'd rather remember Uncle George's studio the way it was,' Beth said. She tried to suppress a shiver. 'I'll help with the washing up. John, you go and choose us one of his paintings. I'll go along with whatever choice you make.'

Hattie showed me the door of the studio and vanished quickly before I could open it. Beth blew me a kiss and followed her. I was left to enter the ruined room on my own. The background scent changed suddenly from old, mellow pipe-smoke to an acrid smell of burned nitrocellulose which suddenly evoked for me a nostalgic memory of the army and long days on the firing range.

It had been a pleasant room, built onto the side of the house with an artist's needs in mind. Tall, north-facing windows and an angled skylight had admitted steady light in daytime and I noticed that the fluorescent lamps were of the type which most nearly simulates the spectrum of daylight. The ceiling, and as much of the walls as were visible, were painted a pale, unobtrusive grey.

One of the windows held plywood where a pane had been blown out, but otherwise the room was as the explosion had left it, complete with some unpleasant stains on the hardwood floor. The force of the blast had gone mainly upward, so that the work-bench which stood opposite the windows was almost undamaged but the ceiling above it was on the point of disintegration.

A low cupboard, which stood like an island in mid-floor beside a large easel, was littered with the paraphernalia of painting. The canvas on the easel showed only a few charcoal lines, but the shape of a river backed by a line of dunes jumped to the eye.

As I moved towards the work-bench, something gritted underfoot. Looking down, I saw that some lead shot, larger than game shot but smaller than BB, had been spilled among the other debris. A briar pipe and a large ashtray lay near the end of the bench beside an overturned stool. Uncle George might have been a canny man when he came to reload, but it seemed that he had allowed himself the occasional pipe in the studio when otherwise engaged. Empty twelve-bore cartridges were scattered around, apparently from a plastic box which had been blown across the room. I picked one of them up. It was a twelve-bore, three inch magnum case. It had been previously fired, as I could tell from the blackening around the crimp, but the percussion cap had already been replaced.

As a former reloader myself, I could make some sense of the scene. Uncle George had already sized and reprimed his cases – that, I thought, was a job which he could do at any time, smoking or not. The next step would have been the loading of the propellant powder, and for that he had sensibly waited until he had finished his postprandial pipe.

The metering out of powder and shot would have been done by means of small measures with spoonlike handles, and for that one needs a broad dish. Beth's uncle had kept his powder in a heavy, cast-iron pot which, charred and slightly deformed, still stood in the middle of the bench. A similar pot standing at the back of the bench, and which was too heavy to have been moved even by the explosion, held shot similar to the pellets on the floor. It had a tightly fitting lid but of thinner metal than the pot, and the shreds of metal scattered throughout the studio suggested that an identical lid on the pot of powder had fragmented. The effect had been like shrapnel. A polythene bag of fibre wads had been blown unopened across the room.

But I had come to look at pictures, not to recreate in my mind the last moments of a well-known artist.

Like many another painter, George Muir had kept a large stock of unsold canvases in hand. With some, he had probably been dissatisfied. Others might have been recently finished or had been held back with some exhibition in mind. Unfortunately, instead of racking them or storing them away he had kept them hanging on hooks from picture rails at three levels. Around and between them were hung the skins of birds and animals, easy sources of reference for colour and texture.

Nearly all the paintings were damaged by smoke or flying metal or both. Worse still, the few paintings which seemed to have escaped had been mere landscapes; competent enough work in their way but without the wildlife which had been his forte. Some of them struck my uneducated eye as definitely mundane. I wondered whether these were early works or background studies waiting for wildlife subjects to present themselves for incorporation.

The other paintings were more to my taste, perhaps because of the gems which they contained rather than for any difference in technique. A badger snuffling beneath rhododendrons. Rabbits playing on a grassy slope. Red deer high on a barren hill. But best of all, the birds. Soaring in mating flight, fleeing, stooping on prey, somehow magically alive and moving against backgrounds which were hazier and yet perfect – scenery that one seemed to know, skies which were dramatic but totally believable.

I had carried my drink with me. I took a long sip while I studied the paintings.

Most of them were badly damaged, ripped by large fragments of metal or peppered by smaller. A magnificent painting of a golden eagle, standing over its egrets and preparing to take off, had escaped the flying splinters and had been only lightly stained by smoke, but had been dislodged from its hook and in falling had impaled itself on a wooden chair back. It was, in any case, too powerful a subject for hanging in the peaceful sitting room at Three Oaks. I would never have relaxed under that painting for fear that the eagle would take me for a threat to its young . . .

I settled at last, as I had known I would, on a painting of geese. One corner had been damaged but the flap of canvas was complete. A few tiny holes resembled those made by death watch beetle, but the beetle does not attack canvas. A day's attention from a competent restorer and the damage would never be seen again. It showed a skein of pinkfeet in a glassy dawn, coming in off an estuary which I thought might be Loch Striven. The skein was unsteady, disturbed and changing direction. There was something about the furthest goose, which perspective had made the smallest. Close up it was only a splodge of half-mixed pigments but when I stood back I saw that it had already been shot and was beginning to fall. From further back still the jumbled colours resolved themselves into the barred chest of a whitefront – a protected species in Scotland although not in the south. Beth's uncle had had a mischievous sense of humour.

While I had been agonising over my choice I had been nagged by inconsistencies in the other picture – my mental one of the fatal accident. Starting with the image of the man in the photograph, I could picture George Muir entering the room, settling on his stool, setting out his box of empty cartridges and pulling forward the pot of powder. Perhaps he had refilled it. I could see the explosion, the flying shrapnel and the artist thrown backwards, horridly mutilated. I could hear the clatter of the broken window pane. Some of the fragments of glass lay inside, on the window sill. The effects of blast often include suction.

But what came between the arrival of George Muir and the explosion? I drifted back to the bench. I was very aware of being a stranger in the silent, ravaged room.

There were no loading tools to be seen. Under one end of the work-bench there was a stack of narrow drawers. The lower drawers held simple woodworking tools. From these and some battens under the bench I inferred that George Muir had made his own stretchers for canvases. An electric grinder bolted to the end of the bench would have been used for sharpening tools. That could certainly have created a whole shower of sparks, which might have triggered the explosion. But it was not easy to picture a sequence which would culminate with the sharpening of a knife or chisel while the powder was uncovered, even if George Muir were to be so careless.

The top drawer held a beautiful set of ivory-handled loading tools, a tin of powder and a bag of shot. There were also a couple of fishing reels and a book of flies. This was George Muir's store for his smaller sporting equipment – guns and rods would be kept elsewhere, probably under lock and key. One of the reels was loaded with nylon line, the end of which was attached to a drawing-pin in the bottom of the drawer. George Muir, I decided, had anchored his line while winding it onto the spool of the reel.

Beth's uncle had lifted the lid of his powder container before rather than after taking out his loading tools. Well, why not?

But where had the spark come from? Any activity involving the bench grinder seemed incompatible with preparations for hand-loading cartridges. And, if the lid had been lifted, how had it come to be blown around like shrapnel? Furthermore, with the lid up the propellant powder would be unconfined and would have burned rather than have exploded. On the other hand, with the lid closed, how would a spark reach the powder?

I was looking down on the bench while I thought about it. A dark line across the pale wood led my eye back to the powder pot. A charred mess still lay in the bottom – burnt powder and something else. I stirred it with my finger and guessed that he had lined the bottom of the pot with paper.

What I had taken to be a fleck of some pale material came into focus and I realised that there was a tiny hole near the bottom of the pot. That could explain a lining of paper. The hole was almost aligned with the dark streak on the bench-top.

But this made little or no sense. The hole was too small for any fuse which I had ever seen. On the other hand, it was as large as the touch-hole in a flintlock. If a flame were led to it from outside . . . But who could light a fuse with reasonable certainty that George Muir would be arriving at his work-bench as the flame reached the powder?

A wife, I decided suddenly. A wife who could see her husband knocking out his evening pipe and preparing to move; and who would know from habit just how long it always took him to reach his bench.

But that would still be uncertain. He might detour to the lavatory, or move quickly and arrive in time to smell the burning fuse and get out of harm's way.

There was another way of looking at it. Suppose somebody had knocked him on the head, inflicting injuries which would be obliterated in the subsequent explosion. Prop him, dead or unconscious, over the pot of explosive. Light the blue touchpaper and retire immediately.

Who? The widow again. The widow, the one person in a position to swear that the explosion had come only seconds after her husband entered the studio, who could brush away any traces remaining of the fuse, who was just not interested in such of her husband's paintings as could be destroyed. She might not have realised that many thousands of pounds would be knocked off the value of her inheritance. Or she might not have cared. George Muir had been selling his paintings for very high figures for a long time and he had lived modestly. He had certainly not died a pauper.

I picked up the stool, perched on it and finished my drink slowly while I thought it over.

The bottom drawer held, among other tools, a mallet and a tack-hammer. Without lifting them I could not detect any traces of blood or skin or hair, but any competent forensic scientist would be able to tell what had last been struck with either of them.

Was it any of my damn business? Yes, I decided, it was. Before my illness I had served Queen and country by killing or attempting to kill whoever was identified as their enemy, so I had no phobias about the sanctity of human life. If he had been a blackmailer or a drug-dealer I would have nodded and gone on my way. But a major talent had been wiped out. It was everybody's business.

Was I sure? No. But I was damned if I could think of a better explanation for all the known facts.

What was I going to do about it? After very little more thought, I decided that the less I said, to Beth or to her aunt by marriage, the better. A quiet word in confidence with the police and I would have done all that was necessary. I could step back and leave it to them, duty done and conscience clear, and nobody need know that I had ever had any suspicions, let alone voiced them. So I thought, in my innocence.

It was very quiet in the room. The darkness outside the uncurtained windows seemed to be full of eyes. I forced myself to relax. I spent another few minutes in tidying the whole problem away to the back of my mind. I still had to get through a weekend with Beth and the widow. So I arranged my features in a smile and carried the large canvas through to the living room.

Three

Beth and Hattie were sitting together and deep in a conversation which they broke off as I entered. I was quite used to such behaviour. Beth's conversations with Isobel were often similarly truncated. Sometimes it was girl talk, but more often the subject was matrimonial probabilities or my state of health.

I propped the picture on a chair and took a seat. I refused tea but accepted another whisky.

My choice of painting was approved by Beth – not that I had the least intention of allowing her to change my mind. Hattie seemed surprised that I had chosen a picture which gave more emphasis to birds than to scenery, but she admitted that the colours were pretty. I wondered how George Muir had managed to sustain a lengthy marriage to a woman whose aesthetic perceptions seemed to have stopped short at the pictures on greetings cards, and decided that he had probably found Hattie a relief. His acquaintances had no doubt felt obliged to discuss Art with him, out of the depths of their ignorance, just when he was sick of his chosen profession and hoping to take his mind off it.

In contrast to Hattie's disinterest, now that I had the painting in my hands I was appreciating it more and more by the minute. Each glance revealed fresh detail. Once I was sure where the solitary wildfowler had to have placed himself, a faint trace across the sand turned itself into a line of footprints. It would have gone against the grain to put the picture back in the studio. There might be other and less scrupulous legatees. 'I'll put it in the car,' I said. 'Then we can leave it with a restorer in Glasgow tomorrow.'

'That would be best,' Hattie agreed. 'There's still young Edgar to make his choice. After that, an agent can uplift the lot and see what's to be done with them and the builders can come in and see to the damage. I shan't be sorry to have the house set to rights.' At the mention of Edgar's name I thought that her nostrils flared slightly, as if at a bad smell.

'We may not need to go right into Glasgow tomorrow,' Beth told me. 'Not unless you want to go to the restorer.' She turned her left hand and held it out. I saw the sparkle of gems on the third finger.

'It was my mother's engagement ring,' Hattie said. She sounded almost shy. 'I'm not one to wear much jewellery. I've no daughter of my own to leave it to and Beth was always her uncle's favourite. George gave me this, so it's a fair exchange.' She showed us her own ring, of two large, square-cut diamonds. The ring on Beth's finger was more modest, a diamond ringed by small rubies, but it was a very pretty ring and far from valueless. It suited Beth's slim young fingers better than anything more ostentatious would have done.

'If you're quite sure,' I said awkwardly, aiming the phrase indiscriminately between the two of them. I was struggling to hide my acute embarrassment. Beth's legacies from her uncle were one thing, but to accept a gift from his widow was quite another.

Logic insisted that Hattie had to be implicated in her husband's death, although the absolute openness of her manner made the idea seem absurd. If there should be any grounds for my suspicions, the ring would have to go back. Meantime, let them both be happy.

'You're sure you don't mind?' Beth asked me.

'Bless you, no. I'm not proud. We can spend the money on the house instead.'

'That's all right, then.' Beth jumped up impulsively and stooped to kiss first Hattie and then myself on the cheek. 'I love the ring and now I'll have something to remember each of you by.'

'Try not to sound as though I'll be gone tomorrow,' Hattie said severely, but I could see that she seemed pleased. She turned on me. 'You'd best be taking that thing out to the car,' she said briskly. 'I'm expecting neighbours in and it's making the place look untidy.'

Telling myself that Hattie's sharpness was no more than her way of hiding a soft heart, I manhandled the painting to the front door. The old Labrador, scenting a walk, began to struggle to her feet but subsided at a word from Hattie. The switch for the light over the front door evaded me. The canvas was too large to go behind the back seat of the estate car. Rather than let it stand in the drizzle which had set in, I left it in the doorway while I laid the back seat flat, fumbling with the catches in the poor illumination of the courtesy light.

I was just laying the painting in place, and feeling for the first time that it might really be ours, when a car came up the drive and parked close to mine, effectively blocking me in. A man got out, leaving his engine running and his lights on. 'What are you doing?' he demanded.

The words were innocent enough, but his tone was suspicious and held all the arrogance of a man who was sure that he had every right to ask insulting questions of complete strangers. It was, in fact, the tone which a landowner might use towards an under-gardener. I found it difficult to see him clearly behind the blazing headlamps but his outline seemed to be distinctly pear-shaped.

His aggression was tainting a moment which I wanted to savour. There had been a time when it took me hours to get angry, but since my illness I seemed to have a much shorter fuse. My hackles, which I usually kept smooth by an effort of conscious restraint, rose on the instant. I chose the politest from four possible replies.

'None of your bloody business,' I said.

Without further comment he reached into his car and began a fanfare on a very loud set of horns.

The light over the front door came on – the switch that had eluded me turned out to be hidden behind one of the coats on the hall stand. Hattie appeared in the doorway with Beth at her side. 'Do stop that noise, Alistair,' Hattie said mildly. 'What do you think you're doing?'

He removed his hand from the horn and switched off his engine. The headlamps died and I saw that he was a large man, tall and with a belly on him. If he had not been obviously male I would have put him down as eight months pregnant. His face was square, jowly, with fleshy lips and an overbearing brow.

Hattie's words must have made it plain that I was no burglar, but he did not seem in the least abashed. 'This chap was loading one of George's paintings into a car in the dark,' he said. 'I thought I'd better check on him. For all I knew, he'd just knocked you on the head.' The accent was meant to be English and educated, but there was just a trace of a glottal stop.

'Well, he has not done any head-knocking yet,' Hattie said, 'and if he has any such intention in mind I don't think that I will be the victim. Don't keep him standing out there in the damp. Come in and be properly introduced.'

'Oh, very well,' the man said ungraciously. 'Come on, Hilda.' He stood, waiting.

The woman who got out of the passenger side was as small as her companion was huge. She elected to come round the front of the car so that I had to move back against my rear door. As she squeezed past me through the gap, I realised that she was even thinner than I was. She gave an impression of weightlessness and even through her artificial fur coat I could feel the hardness of her ribs against my hip. The top of her head failed to reach my chin by at least a hand's breadth.

I finished stowing the painting, locked up the car and followed them into the house. The others were still in the hall. 'This is George's niece, Beth,' Hattie was saying, 'and her fiancé, John Cunningham. *Captain* John Cunningham,' she added, as though that should put my character beyond any possible doubt. 'Mr and Mrs Alistair Young. The Youngs are my nearest neighbours. Now do for Heaven's sake come and have a drink and let there by no more foolish argie-bargies.'

When drinks had been dispensed – whisky for the men, sherry for the ladies and dry-looking cigarettes untouched in a box on the rosewood coffee table – and she had us seated in a neat semi-circle round the fireplace and the blank television set, Hattie decided to explain us to each other.

'Hilda and Alistair were a great help when . . . it happened,' she said. 'They live just a hundred yards further up the hill. Hilda heard the bang— '

'We both did,' Mrs Young said. Her accent was unashamedly Glasgow, but from the better side of it. 'I thought that it was a shot. But Alistair said that if that was a shot he was a monkey's uncle, which of course he isn't— '

'I feel as though I were, sometimes,' Alistair Young said. His look invited sympathy.

' —so we came down straight away. Luckily, my brother was visiting us for the evening with all his brood, so we could leave the children with him.'

Hattie was looking put out at the interruptions. 'I had already called the Emergency Services,' she said. 'I was just sitting by the phone, knowing that I should be doing something but quite unable to think of anything sensible to do. My mind wouldn't accept that George was dead and I could only think of clearing up the mess, but nothing would have dragged me back in there. Then they knocked on the door and called out to ask whether I was all right.'

'Not an easy question to answer,' I said.

Hattie looked at me in surprise. 'You're right,' she said. 'I was dazed, and at first I could only take the question literally. I nearly answered that I was perfectly all right. Then I saw how silly that would be and I went to let them in. I explained that George seemed to have blown himself up.

'They were very kind. Hilda made me drink some whisky and then made tea while Alistair went into the studio. He came back after a few minutes to say that there was no doubt that George was dead, which

I already knew even if I had difficulty accepting it. What I wanted to know most of all was whether there was any danger of fire or of another explosion, but he set my mind at rest.'

'I switched the lights off,' Alistair Young said, 'in case the wiring had taken any damage. That seemed to be the only danger.'

'There wasn't much we could do after that,' his wife added, 'except stay with Hattie and try to keep her occupied until the police arrived. And an ambulance.'

'And very glad I was,' Hattie said. 'I think I'd have gone to pieces, alone in this big house with George dead and myself wondering what had happened and what else might happen. They've been very helpful and attentive ever since.' She looked at me as she spoke. She was explaining, in her own way, why the Youngs should be taking a more than neighbourly interest in her wellbeing.

'The very least we could do,' Alistair Young said modestly.

With the Youngs satisfactorily accounted for, Hattie decided to explain our presence. 'George left Beth the first choice of a painting in his will.'

Alistair Young held out his glass for a refill and chuckled. 'So that's why you were putting a picture into your car in the dark. You only had to say so, young man.'

Evidently he considered our difference to be forgiven and forgotten by both of us, but he was still managing to irritate me. For one thing, he was only a few years older than myself. 'I didn't have to say so,' I pointed out.

There was a quick flash of anger from under the beetling brows. 'All George's best work was cut to pieces,' he said. He sounded not displeased.

'Beth was also left the dog which Edgar has in training,' Hattie said loudly into the sudden silence. 'George was so looking forward to getting him, it's a shame that he couldn't have lived to see the day. There was something missing from his life when Mona became too stiff to work any more. A new dog would have given him a fresh lease of life. He said that this dog would see him out, so he wanted a good one.' She got up and fetched from a side table a pencil sketch in a silver photograph frame. It showed a handsome Labrador pup of about six months, caught in the act of playing with a ball. It had been executed with very few lines and yet it was all there, the individuality of the pup and more. Some of George Muir's hopes for the pup showed through.

'Oh yes. The famous pup,' Young said. There was a hint of tolerant amusement in his voice. 'What was his name again?'

'Jason,' Beth said. 'Luckily, Uncle George hadn't written to the Kennel Club yet, so we can add our kennel name when we register him. Throaks. Short for Three Oaks.'

'I'm sure he'll love that,' Young said.

There was another short and nasty silence. The comfortable room seemed to have lost its friendly atmosphere the moment the Youngs walked into it.

The sketch had been passing from hand to hand and was now with Beth. She put it down carefully on the coffee table. 'What family do you have?' she asked, falling back on the woman's eternal stand-by for bridging awkward gaps in conversation.

Hilda Young brightened immediately. 'Two girls and a boy,' she said. 'There's quite a good school locally, so that's where they go. A boarding school was out of the question.'

'You know we both agreed— ' her husband began.

'We disapprove of private education,' Mrs Young amended quickly. 'And we feel that boarding schools aren't good for the more sensitive children. It's nicer to have them at home, of course, but it does make rather a crush in that wee house.' She glanced apprehensively at her husband.

'We rather hope to be moving soon,' Young said.

'George made a provision in his will,' Hattie said. 'Alistair and Hilda can exchange houses with me, provided that they pay the difference between the two values as estimated by a mutually chosen surveyor. I was agreeable,' she added quickly. 'George consulted me when he made his will. This house will be too big for me on my own, and I'll be fine and happy in the smaller one. It has just the same view over the loch.'

'We'll have a separate dining room again,' Hilda said happily. 'And the girls can have their own bedrooms, which will be a blessing, because we can make them responsible for tidying their own. When you have bairns,' she told Beth, 'never ever let them share a room or you'll find their stuff all over the floor; and whichever of them you tell to pick it up, what do you get? "That isn't mine. I didn't drop it."'

'I'll remember,' Beth said, smiling.

'And Alistair's offered me a hundred pounds for George's old gun,' Hattie said. 'It isn't here, of course. The police are holding it for the moment, because I don't have whatever sort of certificate it is that you need. But that'll answer another little problem.'

I was suddenly suspicious. A hundred pounds does not buy much of a gun. 'Had he had it long?' I asked.

'Since the year dot,' said Young.

'About thirty years, I suppose,' Hattie said. 'He had it made for him in Edinburgh when he was a young man. It was a present from his father. Somebody called Dickson made it. I remember that because Dickson was my maiden name.'

A custom-built Dickson from the 1950s or 1960s would be worth a lot of money unless . . . 'Unless he's backed the car over it or dropped it into salt water—' I began.

'George was aye very careful of his things,' Hattie said seriously.

'Then I think that you should have it valued,' I said.

Alistair Young bristled. 'I hardly think— '

My tongue decided to run away with me. 'Or,' I said, 'if you prefer, I'll give you two hundred for it, sight unseen.'

Young hesitated. He was caught in a trap. If he increased his offer he would be admitting that he had been looking for a thief's bargain. If he agreed to a valuation, the same fact would emerge later but with greater clarity. He took the only way out. 'I am not joining in an auction,' he said with dignity. 'I was only trying to help an old friend out of a tricky situation. My offer is withdrawn. Hattie, I suggest that you accept this young man's rash offer.'

They left shortly afterwards. Hattie saw them to the door. Her manner was apologetic. When she came back she said, 'That wasn't very nice.'

I assumed, perhaps wrongly, that she was referring to my behaviour. 'I'm sorry, but nor was he. And he was trying to rip you off,' I told her.

'I'm not going to fash myself over a few pounds for an old gun.'

I held my peace. If she still wanted to give Alistair

Young a bargain despite my warning, at least she could give it with her eyes open.

An unfortunate chance might have marred our visit.

My physique might be recovering from the years of illness, but my nerves were slower to mend and I was still prey to insomnia, induced by anxieties real or imagined. The squabble with Alistair Young, coming on top of my concern over George Muir's death, had unsettled me. Sleep was slow to come in a strange and lonely bed. I crept through to Beth. We both felt loving, though in a Platonic way, and we soon fell asleep comfortingly entwined.

It would not do for Hattie to find us together, so I set my mental alarm clock for 6.30. Unfortunately that clock, which had never let me down during my army days, had become rusty with disuse. We were woken by Hattie, who brought Beth a cup of tea at eight.

She said nothing at the time, but made a tight-lipped exit. Over breakfast, however, her soft, Highland voice embarked on a contrastingly stern lecture in which religious morality, the physical and psychological dangers of promiscuity and the decline of the younger generation were obscurely mingled.

My view was that 'Least said, soonest mended', and while, from my own confused ethics, I would have disputed the applicability of her sentiments to Beth and myself, I agreed in principle with most of them. I was prepared to listen in respectful silence, but Beth, who never hesitated to read me a lecture of her own, was just as determined that nobody else should ever think ill of me. She broke into Hattie's lecture.

'We won't come back tonight, if you think we've

abused your hospitality,' she said. She was pink but determined. 'We wouldn't want to upset you when you've been so good to us. But nothing happened. John still isn't fit after his illness.'

The last two statements, taken separately, were true. As a single entity, they were misleading to say the least. I could even have resented the implication, except that I was too amused by the truly feminine example of *suppressio veri*.

There is a certain type of West Highlander who is the world's foremost example of double thinking. Strict Sabbatarians and churchgoers, they are scandalised by any example of overt sexuality; yet they are at the same time romantics. Convention seems to be satisfied provided only that marriage takes place before the arrival of the firstborn, following a presumably immaculate conception.

Hattie looked hard at my meatless frame. 'I'm expecting you,' she said. And she refilled my bowl with muesli and made me eat it up. Beth's head was lowered over her egg, but I thought that she was hiding a grin.

That subject, clearly, was now closed. Something else was troubling Hattie. 'Alistair Young went back a long way with George,' she said.

'If he's a friend of yours, I'm sorry,' I said. Then I realised that my words were unintentionally double edged and I hurried on. 'If I was out of line, forget what I said. But he did go out of his way to put my hackles up.'

'He seems that way, sometimes.' Hattie paused and shook her head. 'Truth to tell, I've no great fondness for the man myself and I could do without his being quite so possessive. But the two of them have been a help to me and I'm sorry for Hilda. I feel I owe it to George to keep in wi' any friends of his.'

'I understand,' I said. 'Don't fret over it.'

'I doubt that you do,' she said unhappily. 'I know that he did George a big favour in the past. And never let him forget it. But I thought at least that I could trust the man.' She paused in the act of forcing more toast on me. I think that she would have spread it and cut it up into soldiers if I had allowed her. 'Did you mean what you said about George's old gun?'

I said that I did.

'Write me a cheque for two hundred, then, and it's yours.'

'But I could probably get you more,' I protested.

'You didn't mean it, then?'

Beth was avoiding my eye but I thought that she was hiding another smile. I am a non-gambler by nature, but Hattie had saved us as much or more by the gift of her ring. And I could always sell my old gun to cover the expense. I had a chequebook in my pocket. I wrote her a cheque.

'You write me a note confirming the sale,' I said, 'so that I can get it from the police.'

'Aye,' she said. 'I'll do that.'

'Wouldn't you rather that I sold it for you in Glasgow?'

'I just want the whole thing settled. I'm happy to be rid of the worry of it.'

She came out to the car with us when we left. 'Be back by six,' she said. 'If, by any chance, I'm out, look for the key on the ledge above the door. I may be walking with Mona. She likes to be taken by the ways where George used to go with her. Drive carefully, now.'

She stood back and waved as we started down the hill. It was a sharp, clear morning. The view eastward over the loch was truly superb. I could understand why she would want to keep the view, with or without the house. I had glimpsed the Youngs' house from my bedroom window. It looked neat and rather prim in the morning sun.

The police from Arrochar had dealt with George Muir's death. I drove there, found the police station on the main road and slipped the car into a parking space.

'You just can't wait to find out whether your bet's come off,' Beth said.

'You don't mind waiting for a minute?'

'Well, I've got my ring.' She stretched out her hand to admire it again. 'I can't grudge you a new toy. Run along and enjoy yourself. I rather hope you've picked up a bargain, just to show Hattie that Mr Young's a nasty piece of work.'

'I rather think that she knows it.'

In fact, preoccupied as I was with my worries over her uncle's demise, until Beth spoke I had relegated the gun to a recess at the back of my mind. It was probably a pitted old relic belonging on the wall above the painting of the geese. I smiled and got out of the car.

A civilian clerkess was in charge of the desk. She fetched a grey-haired sergeant to attend to me.

It seemed easiest to start with the gun. I produced Hattie's written confirmation of my purchase and, from my wallet of credit and bank cards, my own shotgun certificate. He fetched a bagged gun and I signed a receipt.

'There's another thing,' I said lamely. He waited, polite and helpful, not even looking at me. A woman had come in to complain about a neighbour's cats. 'It should be confidential,' I said.

He took me into a small interview room and we settled in hard chairs. He seemed to be absorbed in a poster which advised interviewees of their rights. 'Can you tell me who investigated George Muir's death?' I asked.

That woke him up all right. He looked straight at me for the first time, but his politeness never faltered. 'I was called to the scene,' he said, 'I phoned in that it was clearly an accident and followed it up with a written report. A CID sergeant came out from Stirling to confirm it. His report to the procurator fiscal must have agreed, because the fiscal didn't order an enquiry. Does that answer your question? Now suppose you tell me what your interest is.'

'I hope very much that your report was absolutely correct,' I said. 'But I have my doubts and I thought that it was my duty to let you know.'

As I explained my involvement and ran over the reasons for my disquiet, he turned a dull red and I could see him stiffening. 'You have little enough to go on,' he said. He seemed to be one of the old school, yet he was in no hurry to call me sir. For him, the form of address had to be earned.

'Perhaps you're right,' I said. 'In your report, did you suggest that the lid was on the pot when the explosion happened?'

His eyes went out of focus as he thought back. 'I don't think that I touched on it,' he said at last. 'But from the way the fragments flew around, the lid must have been in place.'

'Then you might have wondered how a spark managed to get in. Or did you notice that a tiny hole had been made in the pot?'

'I did not.' He paused, holding my eyes with his own. 'It's my experience that you can never explain every smallest circumstance of a fatal accident. Folk do the damnedest things, you see. Assuming that you're right, what do you propose to do with this information?' he asked coldly.

'Not a damn thing. I had doubts. I've told the police about them. Now I'd like to forget it. And if any more steps are taken, I'd prefer that my name was left out of it. Good day to you.' I got up and began to walk out. That would be the end of it as far as I was concerned. The dignity of my exit was spoiled when he had to call me back to collect the forgotten gun.

Back at the car, I handed the bagged gun to Beth and dropped into the driver's seat.

'Well?' she said. 'Is it any good? Or was Alistair Young right after all? From your face . . . '

'I haven't even looked at it yet,' I said. 'I didn't feel external hammers, so it's probably less than a hundred years old.'

'Don't you think you should look?'

I put George Muir's death out of my mind and remembered that I had a present to open. That it was a present from myself robbed it of none of its surprise. 'Yes,' I said. 'You're right. But not in a public street. They'd think I had my eye on the bank.'

'What took you the time?' Beth asked. 'I thought you must have taken it to bits and be going over it with a microscope.'

'Formalities,' I said. I got the car moving and turned back towards Tarbet.

'What is it about men and guns?' Beth asked. 'You never look so perked up when I buy you a present. I thought you'd be sick of guns, after fighting in the army.'

'The shotgun's something different,' I said. 'An old armourer once pointed it out to me. A shotgun's designed to come naturally to the shoulder and point where you're looking. It's the one object in the world which has every part of every surface placed perfectly to suit either its function or the human frame and hands. Add to that that it's the product of around six hundred years of gradual refinement.'

'Isobel says that it's a phallic symbol,' Beth said.

'Maybe she's right. Or maybe I'm just harking back to the small boy playing cowboys and Indians. But to me, a good gun is the supreme human artifact. A bad one's an insult to human intelligence.'

I got us onto the road for Glasgow, stopped in a layby and drew the gun out of its bag – an awkward manoeuvre in the confines of the car. While I was driving, I had prepared myself for a disappointment. Hattie could have been wrong and so could I. George Muir might have bought himself a much older and cheaper gun and have had it altered to fit him by Dickson.

What I took out was a Dickson Round Action, apparently in mint condition. The bores were mirror-perfect, the blueing unblemished and the stock was of best walnut, oil-polished to a subtle gloss.

'Bloody hell!' I said.

Beth's nose was almost making smears on the engraving. 'What is it?' she asked. 'Artifact or insult? It looks all right. I don't think you were done. Uncle George liked good things.'

'I wouldn't have been done if I'd put another nought on the end,' I said. 'This is valuable. What on earth do I do now?'

'What would you have done if it had turned out to be rubbish?' Beth asked.

I bagged the gun again, twisted round to lay it very carefully beside the picture in the rear and got us back on the road. 'I think I'd have decided that it served me right for shooting my mouth off.'

'Right. But you made an offer, sight unseen. You warned Hattie. And you paid her twice what she'd been prepared to accept. Make an excuse to do Hattie an extra favour some time. But keep the gun, enjoy it and shut up worrying.'

Since that was exactly what I wanted most in the world to do, Beth's common sense found an eager response in me. Even so, I knew that it would be years before I would be able to look Hattie in the eye again.

The improvements to the A82 had made the run past Balloch and Dumbarton seem much shorter if less scenic than when the road had switchbacked and twisted along the lochside. We entered Glasgow by Dumbarton Road, left the car in a multi-storey carpark and walked the rest of the way. I was struggling with the painting, which had a tendency to act as a sail in the fitful breeze, and Beth had the gunbag slung over her shoulder. Beth grumbled both at the weight and at the curious glances which we both drew; but I was not leaving the gun behind. Cars are too easily entered and there are no hiding places in the average estate car.

The only picture restorer known to me had a shop in a small street just outside the city centre. I had visited him occasionally over the restoration of some regimental portraits and, when I came out from behind the painting, he recognised me immediately.

'Captain Cunningham!' he said. 'This is a pleasure.'

'Mister Cunningham now, Mr Grogan,' I said.

'Invalided out several years ago. But it's good to see you again. Personal business this time, not regimental.' I introduced him to Beth and he smiled at her as if deciding that her complexion could do without rebacking.

He tutted over the damage to the George Muir painting, but admitted that it would yield to his magic. I could collect it in a fortnight, framed just as we wanted it.

'Terrible thing, him being killed that way,' he said when our business was concluded. 'Very sad. You've seen the studio? How bad is the damage?'

His concern would not be for the building. 'I was there last night,' I said. 'And it's bad. Some of the paintings are almost shredded. Most have rips in them. Mrs Muir intends to get an agent to uplift the best of them. I was wondering whether to suggest that somebody like yourself advised her first.'

'Without a doubt,' he said. 'That's what the agent would do, and he'd put his own profit onto my work.'

'Give me your card,' I said. 'I'll pass it on to her. If she cares to follow it up, you can give her a quotation.'

'Aye,' he said soberly. 'It'll not be cheap. But it'd be money well spent, even on the worst damaged of them. His pictures'll take a big jump in value now that he's awa'. There'll be no more, you see. Not ever.' He paused and lowered his voice. 'You could trust my discretion regarding anything out of the ordinary.'

'I'm sure we could,' Beth said. She tugged at my sleeve.

We left the gun in his care and went for lunch.

'What was Grogan talking about?' I asked Beth. '"Anything out of the ordinary"?'

'I haven't the faintest idea,' she said. 'All Uncle George's work was out of the ordinary. But I expect your Mr Grogan knows what he's doing.'

Four

Edgar Lawrence lived in the agricultural fringe between Glasgow's peripheral industries and the Lennox Hills. We went out through Bearsden and followed the instructions he had given to Beth over the phone. These brought us through alternating strips of prosperity and industrial decay, until we arrived at a narrow and potholed road through landscape which still bore the scars of earlier quarrying or opencast mining, long since defunct and now mostly overgrown. It was a backwater, not affluent but not displeasing.

We found a row of four brick cottages, once workmen's dwellings but now forced up-market by the pressures from the city. The same pressure would eventually force their conversion into one or two houses of more respectable size, with colour-washed walls, cedar panels and double glazing, but for the moment, as we could see by the doors and fences, they were still as poky and utilitarian as when they had been built.

We draped coats over the gun and locked the car up carefully. According to the numbering, Edgar occupied the gable cottage at the nearer end, but a hearty rat-tat with a rusty knocker brought no response except for some disinterested barking from beyond the house.

The front door of the adjoining cottage gritted open and a woman put her head out and then emerged cautiously. She was thin but with enormous hips. I thought that she was not as young as her style of dress would have had us believe, nor her hair as blonde; but I supposed that I was being unfair. Most women looked secondhand to me beside Beth's freshness.

'Was you wanting Mr Lawrence?' she asked. Her metallic accent would have sounded abrasive, even coming from a Clydeside docker.

My first impulse was to point out that we would hardly have been knocking at his door if we had not wanted him, but Beth jabbed me with her elbow. 'That's right,' she said.

The woman frowned. 'He was expecting his cousin.'

'That's me,' Beth said.

The woman frowned again and then her face cleared. 'I mind now, Edgar said as you was a grown woman but looked like a teeny-bopper. He had a call to go back to his work. He asked me to take you round to have a keek at your wee dog. I'm Jeannie McLaine.'

She led us round the gable of the terrace and through a small garden where some trouble had been taken and mostly wasted on vegetables which had bolted to seed. Edgar's kennels, a row of small sheds, sturdy but ill-matched, each with a tiny, earth-floored run enclosed by wired mesh, stood in the corner of a scrubby field.

'Your dog's in the first kennel, Edgar said. He left out dummies, in case you wanted to try him.'

The name Jason was chalked over the entry to the first run we came to. It held a small, black

Labrador. I was conscious of a sense of disappointment. The sudden acquisition of a George Muir painting, an engagement ring and an excellent shotgun had evoked the spirit of childhood Christmas, encouraging me to expect something rather special. On this trip down the chimney, however, Santa had failed to live up to his previous record. This animal was rather narrow in the head and long legged. Beauty is not a prerequisite in the working dog. Arbitrary and sometimes ill-advised standards set by the Kennel Club had caused show-dog strains to drift away, in size and form, from the dogs bred for work; but the show and working strains had become less separated in the Labrador than in perhaps any other breed and it was quite common to see Labradors competing at field trials which would not have been out of place in the show ring.

Beth, putting aside her chagrin at being likened to a teeny-bopper, opened the gate of the pen and the dog came out willingly enough, glad to be free of the confinement of the run. Other dogs were standing against the mesh, hoping for a walk, food or some other break in the monotony. While I strolled along the row of kennels, Beth walked her dog, trying him at heel. He seemed, at first glance, to be nervous but steady.

There was no name on the furthest run. The run was empty and the door of the shed was closed and latched. I glanced back. The woman was watching me uncertainly. Beth was putting her dog through some simple exercises. It was an ungainly mover, but fast. I ducked through the entry to the run and unlatched the door of the kennel. Another Labrador emerged, stretching, and nosed my hand.

To somebody unused to dogs, one of any breed

may look very like any other; but when you live and work with them, their faces and builds and movements become as individual as those of people and often more so. My suspicions crystallised and I called to Beth.

'Come over here.'

She brought the other dog over and sat him outside the run. He was obedient, but you can teach a Labrador anything short of how to make tea.

'You've got the wrong dog,' I said. 'That one's snipe-headed. No way did the pup your uncle drew grow into that thing. How old is he supposed to be?'

'Eleven months.'

'That dog looks twice that age. Now look over here.' I nodded toward the dog in the pen. He shuffled uneasily, aware that he was being discussed but unable to understand. He was going to develop into a very handsome animal. 'This one's about the right age, and he's exactly what the dog in your uncle's drawing would have grown into.'

The woman, Jeannie McLaine, had come closer. 'I don't know about this,' she said. It was almost a whine. 'I only know what Edgar said. He said your dog was in the first kennel.'

'But from which end?'

'Jason's name was chalked up,' Beth said doubtfully.

'That could be months old,' I said. 'Your cousin could have forgotten about it. Let's give him the benefit of the doubt. There's not another dog here that comes near the right age or build. Have you seen Jason's pedigree?'

'I have it here.' Beth fumbled in her coat pocket. 'Uncle George kept it and Hattie sent it on to me.'

One glance was enough for me. 'His grandsire in the male line was Farthingale Bonus, who has a head like the front of a bus. None of his line ever threw a narrow-headed pup. Look at Joe Little's dogs if you don't believe me.'

'I believe you. Uncle George didn't much like the looks of Edgar's bitch, but he liked the way she worked,' Beth said slowly. She was half convinced and wanted to go the rest of the way. 'He paid the stud fee for a dog that he fancied, in exchange for the choice of pup. Edgar must have sold the rest of the litter. This chap's going to be a beauty.' She stopped and sighed.

If I had harboured any thoughts of taking advantage of the dubiety to discourage Beth, her sigh would have changed my mind for me. 'He is,' I said.

'Isn't there any way we can be sure?'

'Tests would take time,' I said. 'I'm sure enough now.'

'But— '

I made an impatient movement and both dogs jumped back. 'Your cousin's a heavy-handed trainer,' I said in explanation. 'I've even seen him punish a dog in front of the judges. It was only a flick with the leash but I'm sure it cost him a place. Under the new rules he'd have been put out on the spot.' I snapped my fingers gently and the dog I was sure was Jason came to me. I felt his joints and looked into his eyes. He stood patiently still for me, his tail moving slowly. 'We're taking this one with us,' I told Jeannie McLaine, 'before Mr Lawrence ruins him altogether.'

'But I don't know as I should let you— '

'You have no authority to stop us. Please listen very carefully,' I said. 'I want you to give Edgar a message. We think that he nearly made an honest mistake. This one is Jason and we're taking him with us. Edgar can keep the balance of the training fee. If he doesn't like it he can take us to court, in which case we'll have his genetic fingerprint taken.'

'Would that be a blood test like?' she asked, trying to understand.

'Much more specific than a blood test. It can establish parentage without any doubt. But it'd cost, and a court would certainly expect the loser to pay for it. I wouldn't recommend him to try it unless he's absolutely certain. Have you got that?'

She nodded. She looked solemn, but my last doubts were swept away when I detected a glint of hidden amusement in her eye. She was not sorry that Edgar's attempt to commit a fraud while hiding behind her skirts had misfired.

We returned the first dog to his kennel. Jason came with us, puzzled but trusting. He jumped into the back of the car of his own accord and settled down immediately, comforted by the scent of a hundred or so contented dogs who had been there before him.

Jeannie McLaine made a token protest, but her heart was not in it. She stood and watched us out of sight. At the last moment, she waved.

'Your cousin was trying it on,' I said as I drove. 'He hoped you'd go off with the wrong one.'

'I'm afraid so.' Beth turned in her seat to fondle the dog's head. I watched in the mirror. He was pretending to nibble her fingers. 'When we were younger, Edgar always seemed to get his own way, by hook or by crook. And he usually managed to make it look as if it was somebody else's fault. I think he left his girlfriend in charge so that he could blame it on her stupidity if we made any trouble.'

Whatever my own belief, I had no wish to drive a wedge between the cousins. 'Perhaps he really was called back to work,' I said charitably. 'And I don't think you've any grounds for suggesting that she's his girlfriend? He could sue.'

Beth laughed happily. Her first doubts were giving way to elation. 'Edgar was never fussy,' she said. 'And he's an administrative officer with the GPO. I think he keeps the personnel records or something. What kind of emergency would need his attendance on a Saturday? Oh, never mind Edgar. Do you think this fellow's going to turn out well?'

'He'll be a good-looking dog,' I said. 'Just how good he'll be in competition depends on you now.'

'I didn't have a chance to try him.' Beth leaned further over to take a good look at her new friend. A pink tongue flicked out, quick as an adder's strike. 'Ugh! I'm covered in dog-slobber. Back, back, you foul beast!' She sighed deeply with happiness. 'It's turning out to be quite a weekend. A new dog and a ring and a picture and your gun. I keep wondering what's going to go wrong.'

That brought her uncle's death back into my mind and I felt a chill up my back.

'You're looking tired,' Beth said suddenly. 'Would you like me to drive?'

I let the car slow. 'Do you want to?'

'Not really. I don't want to take my eyes off Jason, in case he disappears.'

I would cheerfully have headed for home, taking our treasures with us. Once they were home, they would really be ours. But Hattie was expecting us for another night, while Isobel and Henry would have suspected a lack of trust if we had hurried back to the kennels. So we returned, through Drymen and Balloch, to the house above Tarbet.

The house was locked and empty, but the key was above the door and an appetising smell of roasting meat met us in the hall. Old Mona was missing from her place in front of the hearth, so we guessed that the two of them were out walking. Dusk was on the way, but there was still adequate light. Beth took a pair of canvas dummies out of the car and led Jason onto Hattie's lawn. I left them to get on with it. Instead, I carried the Dickson up to my bedroom, spent a minute or two admiring the Celtic engraving and then practised mounting it to my shoulder. The balance was good and it seemed to fit me perfectly. When I opened and closed it, the action was tight, firm as a safe door and yet sweet and gentle as silk pants.

The sudden knock at my door had to be Hattie; Beth and I had both stopped bothering to knock since our intimacy became established. I had a mad impulse to hide the gun, but laid it carefully across a chair and opened the door.

Hattie came in, still in her winter tweed coat. She glanced at the gun without more than casual interest. 'Beth says that you're unhappy about your bargain.'

Not knowing what to say I held my tongue.

'You've no need to fash yourself,' she said firmly. 'A deal's still a deal, at least in Scotland.' She smiled at me for the first time and I was suddenly reminded of a George Muir portrait which I had seen in an exhibition, a painting of a younger woman with the same dark hair and sturdy grace. 'We don't go in for that gazumping business here. And I've got more than I was expecting for it. If you're happy then I'm contented. Come down when you're ready.' She nodded and left the room.

I breathed again. I had been sure that she was going to ask me to pay the full value or to give the gun back. I was in no position to do the first and could not have brought myself to do the second. 'I'll be down in a minute,' I said to her departing back. It crossed my mind to wonder whether George Muir had not had any other luxury items which his widow wanted to dispose of on similarly favourable terms.

The front doorbell rang as I reached the bottom of the stairs. Hattie and Beth were in the kitchen. I could hear Beth chattering on about her dog. Her tone soared in a way which only happened when she was ecstatic, so I gathered that Jason had performed to her satisfaction. I called out that I would answer the door.

There was a large and very expensive looking BMW standing empty nearby, making my car look old and shabby. The man on the doorstep was small, fortyish and dapper. His cheekbones made his thin face look oddly triangular. When he removed a dark hat, not one greying hair was out of place.

'Is Mr Muir at home?' he asked. When I gaped at him, he said, 'I'm sorry to call without an appointment.'

'Mr Muir died about three weeks ago,' I said. 'Didn't you know?'

'I've been abroad.' He fell silent, understandably unsure how to go on.

He had my sympathy. I would have been lost for words after a facer like that. 'Can I help you at all?' I asked.

'He was painting my dog, from sketches and photographs. A red setter. My name's Fullerton, by the way. Bruce Fullerton. Do you know whether he finished it?'

'You'd better come inside and speak to Mrs Muir,' I said. As I led him towards the living room, Beth's head popped out of the kitchen door. 'Tell Hattie that there's a visitor. I think she should come through.'

In the living room, the two Labradors were curled up together. Mona looked disgusted at the familiarity but too stiff or lazy to move. Jason got up and, recognising a familiar scent, came to me, wagging his tail with such violence that his whole body snaked. I gave Mr Fullerton a chair and sat down opposite him. 'We've met before,' I said.

'I was beginning to think that there was something familiar about you,' he said.

Recollection came to me. 'And I can tell you where. I was picking up on Lord Craill's estate about a year ago. You were a guest on the shoot. But you didn't have a red setter with you.'

Fullerton smiled grimly. 'He's decorative rather than functional, but I've a soft spot for him all the same. And you're the spaniel man. Captain . . . Cunningham, right?'

'Just Mister,' I said. 'I'm out of the army now, and Captain makes me feel as if I'm pretending to be nautical, or to pilot an aircraft.'

He nodded. 'I'll remember, if we meet again. We well might. I live less than ten miles from you.'

Jason, finding that he had lost my attention, gave Fullerton a disinterested sniff and rejoined Mona.

I had heard Hattie's voice giving Beth instructions for the final touches to the meal. She came in then and we both rose. 'This is Mr Fullerton,' I said. 'Another Fifer.'

They shook hands and we sat. 'I'm sorry to hear about your husband,' he said. He was looking at Hattie as though something about her had surprised him. 'He'll be a loss, and not just to yourself. And I'm sorrier to be bothering you at such a time. But he was to do a portrait of Rufus, my red setter. It should have been finished weeks ago, but I've been abroad and this was my first chance to come for it.'

'Oh dear,' Hattie said. 'This is awful!' She sat very still.

'I went through the paintings yesterday,' I explained. 'Most of them are damaged. Mr Muir died in an explosion.'

'If it isn't too badly damaged—' Fullerton began.

'You don't understand,' I said. 'There was no red setter among them.'

Hattie stirred. 'What I was going to say was that there is a portrait. A woman came for it several weeks ago. She said that it was her dog and that the portrait had been paid for. I told her to go and take it and she came back with a painting of a red setter.'

'You didn't get a name?' I asked her.

'No. There was no need,' she said. 'George had said that there'd be somebody coming for it.'

'A name wouldn't help,' Fullerton said. 'I can guess who took it.'

For some unfathomable reason, he looked uncomfortable. I decided to get him out of there before he upset Hattie. 'There are some sketches on a table in the studio,' I said. 'There might be something in there.'

Some of his gloom lifted. 'Do you think so? And there should be the photographs Mr Muir was working from.'

'Come through,' I said.

I looked at Hattie and she nodded.

I led the way to the studio. It took an effort to push the door open.

Bruce Fullerton was sharp. He sniffed the air, in which the smell of smoke still lingered, and stooped to pick up one of the scattered cartridges. 'Mr Muir was reloading cartridges?' he asked.

'It seems so.'

'I suppose the police took away his loading machine.'

'He was hand-loading.'

Fullerton nodded. 'Not a good time to have accidents.'

It seemed unlikely that George Muir had ever thrown away a sketch. A card table in the corner of the room had escaped the flying fragments although some pellets were rolling around on top of the paper. The table was heaped with pencil drawings, photographs and simple water-colours, many of them with scribbled reminders about shades and tones and movement in a firm, neat hand. Some of the wildlife drawings were annotated with geometrical sketches intended to remind the artist of the anatomical proportions of his subject. A tea-chest under the table was almost filled with similar material. I guessed that when the heap on the table neared collapsing point he transferred much of it to the box.

Fullerton began to sort through the upper layers, but my attention was on something else. 'When you met Mrs Muir,' I said, 'you seemed surprised.'

He looked round at me. He had a disconcerting habit of turning his head sharply but only following with the eyes a second or two later. 'She isn't what I thought the wife of a successful painter would be. I was expecting flamboyant clothes – large beads and teeth to match – rather than a big-boned Highlander with domesticity written all over her. Ah, here we are!' he said suddenly. He had unearthed two photographs of a very nice-looking red setter. They were clipped to a small bunch of pencil sketches which showed the same dog in motion and again twining itself around a disembodied leg. Animation and zest came through the pencil lines more surely than through the photographs. The economy and precision of the pencil lines were still an amazement to me.

'I'm glad to have these,' Fullerton said. 'My favourite sister chose him for herself when he was a pup. When she knew that she was dying, she asked me to take him. He came to mean a lot to me. He had one of the nicest natures . . . '

It seemed curious to me that he used the past tense. 'You could take more photographs,' I said.

'I'm afraid not.' He continued scanning down through the pile of sketches while he spoke, never looking up. 'I may as well explain. My wife and I had a fight just before I went abroad. I'm the UK sales manager for an American concern. We have a depot in Glenrothes, so Fife suits me down to the ground. I only wish my private life had worked out as neatly.

'I had to spend several weeks in the States to learn about a new line of products. While I was over there, the quarrel continued by phone. She lost her temper completely and told me that she was going to have the dog put down. I hoped that it was no more than an empty threat . . .

'The next that I heard was that she'd been killed in an accident. Falling downstairs, of all the silly ways to go. I hurried back as soon as I could. There was no trace of the dog. Whether she carried out her threat or just gave him away, I don't know. Perhaps he's in a dogs home somewhere, waiting to be put down if nobody claims or adopts him. I haven't been able to find a trace of him, so it's probably too late.'

'I'm sorry,' I said, more in apology rather than condolence. It was inadequate, but what could I say? I had never been married. I suspected that one could go off a wife. But I knew the lasting affection that one could develop for a dog, which has fewer ways of getting on one's nerves and can always be shut away in times of crisis.

Fullerton left shortly after that and I went with Beth to attend to the feeding of Jason. He wolfed down the meal borrowed from old Mona. The change of scene and owner did not seem to have affected his appetite, but Labradors are notorious gluttons.

Later that night, after I had shaken off the depression induced by the perfidy of Edgar Lawrence and of Bruce Fullerton's wife, Beth and I were both wrapped in the glow which comes with rich and undeserved gifts. This time, we abused Hattie's hospitality to good effect. For each of us it was a giving rather than a taking and it was the most tender experience in the world. Life, I knew suddenly, had turned the corner. It was going to be good again.

We left for home the next morning. Hattie was preparing herself for church and invited us to stay and attend the service with her. I would have liked to oblige her, either in thanks for her kindnesses or in apology for my suspicions. But my belief in a divine being was too precarious to withstand the rigours of organised religion, simplistic concepts, solemn faces, discordant singing and the smell of peppermints. We gave thanks instead to Hattie, from whom all blessings seemed to have flowed, and headed for home. A weight lifted off me as we left behind all suspicions of murder and double dealing.

We lunched at a wayside hotel. There was to be a

clay pigeon meeting at New Gilston and I was sorely tempted to call in and try out the Dickson. But Beth wanted to get home and not even the argument that it would be a good chance to test Jason's response to gunfire would change her mind. She might have a dog of her own now, but it was not in Beth's nature to rest easy until she had satisfied herself as to the safety and wellbeing of her usual charges.

About half a mile beyond our village, we swung left into the drive at Three Oaks. It was only mid-afternoon but the sun, already low, had been swallowed by advancing clouds and the lights of the old house stood out against the dark hill behind, welcoming us home. With the recollection of Edgar Lawrence's cramped and scruffy sheds in my mind I had sweated under a silly fear that our own facilities were no better, that somehow I had been remembering them in the rosy light of proprietary pride. The clean lines of the kennels and runs, away to our left in the shelter of the oaks which gave the place its name, were a reassurance.

Beth was out of the car and away towards the kennels, with Jason at heel and curious, before Isobel emerged to greet us.

'All well?' I asked Isobel.

'No more than the usual minor traumas. Poplar trod on some glass. It didn't need stitches, but she'll be out of training for about ten days. And Brockleton's started dropping the dummy on the way back. Otherwise no problems.'

I sighed. The light was too far gone to start a training session. 'I'll sort Brockleton out tomorrow.'

'You'd better. His owner expects to collect him next week. Now come inside, relax and tell us all about it.' When I glanced towards the kennels, she humphed at me. 'I've told you. They're all fighting fit. There's tea in the pot and I'm making dinner for all of us.'

'The puppies— ' I began.

'Have been fed. The dogs' main meal is prepared. The runs were clean up to half an hour ago.'

'But— '

'Watch my lips,' she snorted. 'There is nothing useful you can do – except maybe help with the feed in about an hour's time. I see that you let Beth bring us another mouth to feed.'

'You know how it is,' I said. 'I can never resist Beth.'

'You can never resist a dog,' Isobel said.

'Who always stops the car if she sees a mongrel with a limp?' I retorted.

Isobel humphed and turned away, but I knew that she was hiding a smile. I slung the gunbag over my shoulder, picked up the cases and followed her into the house.

Life at Three Oaks tended to centre around the large room which, in addition to all the usual features of a kitchen, comfortably housed a dining table and chairs, two easy chairs, the only television set and the central heating boiler. Beth had chosen and together we had carefully hung a suitable and very expensive paper, but this was now next to invisible behind an accumulation of hung plates, dangling utensils and shelves of spices and cookery books. It was a cluttered, homely room. A door at one end led into the hall beyond which was a formal sitting room. At the other end of the kitchen was what we called, illogically, the back door although it was to the front of the house. Beyond that, an outhouse contained most of our stores plus the small room from which we sold books, baskets and training aids to the customers. It had never seemed sensible to send somebody away with a new puppy and not even a lead to go with it.

Henry Kitts, Isobel's husband, looked up from some papers scattered across the table. I gathered that he had been conscripted into helping Isobel with the accounts. Henry was elderly. His face had slipped with the years so that the pouches under his eyes continued as folds in his cheeks, ending up as dewlaps under his jaws. But his tall frame was still so spry that one tended to forget his age. He had long since retired from a business career. Although he had no direct connection with the kennels he took a keen interest in our affairs and was a ready source of help in times of difficulty – and interference on our better days.

Henry had been a shooting man and was still happy to potter around with a gun. His eyes settled immediately on the gunbag. 'Been spending your profits?' he suggested.

'Not very willingly,' I said, 'and not very much. A neighbour was trying to con the widow. He'd offered her a hundred quid for George Muir's old gun, which was still in the hands of the local cops. She didn't believe me when I told her that she ought to have it valued. So I offered her two hundred for it, sight unseen. She took me up on it.'

'You shouldn't be able to lose much, at two hundred,' Henry said. 'Or did you manage that extraordinary feat?'

'Judge for yourself,' I said.

He unfolded his considerable length from the chair and undid the buckle on the bag. When he pulled out the gun, his eyes widened. 'I'll give you four,' he said.

'Come on, now. A hundred per cent mark-up in a few hours. That can't be bad.'

Isobel looked round from pouring tea. 'Henry,' she said, 'are you sure you know what you're doing?'

'He knows,' I said. 'Nice try, Henry.'

'No harm trying.' He mounted the gun to his shoulder. 'I've always thought the Round Action was the prettiest gun ever made. It's heavier than I expected, or else I'm growing feeble.'

'Three inch chambers,' I said, 'and proved for three and a half tons.'

He knew what that meant all right. Such heavy loads are used for wildfowling. 'God! You're not going to take this beauty near salt water?'

'We'll see,' I said. 'If I don't have the heart, the extra weight will suit clay pigeons.'

He swung the gun, endangering the light fitting. 'George Muir may have wanted it for wildfowling,' he said. 'But what they've built for him was their live pigeon, trapshooting gun. And very nice too.'

I locked the gun away in my gun-safe behind the shop. When I came back, Beth was showing Isobel her ring. Henry was making a fuss of Jason, who was concerned to ensure that the time for his dinner did not pass unremembered.

Over cups of tea and while Isobel put our dinner into the oven, we recounted the high spots of the weekend. I said nothing about my suspicions. I was already regretting my rash words to the local sergeant.

Isobel, who began her working life as a vet, was examining Jason. As I had done, she felt his hips and looked deep into his eyes and she seemed satisfied. 'Is this perisher going to be any good?' she asked.

'I haven't had much of a chance to try him,' Beth

said. 'He marks well and he's very biddable but he's not been gently trained.'

'That I can believe,' Isobel said. 'I've seen your cousin competing. All voice and bluster. God alone knows how he made up a champion – he must have had a headache that day. And he argues with the judges, which is always a mistake. Never argue with idiots,' she told Beth. 'It's their privilege to be wrong.'

Beth looked at me shyly. 'If I find that he works well for me, do you think that I could enter him for something soon? The local Association runs retrievers and spaniels in the same two-day event. I could have a trial run and still be Isobel's chauffeur-gopher.'

'Don't try and run too soon,' I said. 'Remember, retrievers don't hunt, so the judges expect much higher standards of steadiness and retrieving. If you're ready, we'll put him in for something after Christmas. I don't think you could get him registered any sooner than that. Don't fret. He'll still be young enough for Puppy Stakes during the first part of next season.'

'I suppose so,' Beth said.

I hated to see her disappointment. An idea came to me. 'There's no better training than picking-up,' I said. 'I'm going to be the only picker-up on Lord Craill's shoot next Saturday. If, and only if, Jason seems good enough, you can bring him along and work him.'

Beth lit up. 'I'd love to.' Her face fell again. 'But Isobel's running Gargany that day.'

'I can drive myself,' Isobel said cheerfully.

She could. But, as we all knew but as Isobel preferred to forget, she could get carried away in the post-trial junketing. When that happened, she could arrive home blotto or not at all. And Henry, who anyway had almost given up driving, was as easily led astray. For a couple who between them had more than a century on the clock, they could sometimes, when the mood took them, be as irresponsible as children.

'It's comparatively local,' I said. 'We can send you by taxi. Or drop you off and pick you up again.'

'Dropping me three hours before the trial begins and then griping at me because you have to wait around for me afterwards,' Isobel said. 'Thank you very much.'

'We'll work something out,' I said.

Beth and I went out into the darkness together, to feed the dogs by the light of the lamps over the runs. As Isobel had said, the dogs were in fine fettle. We fed Jason in one of the pens as a start to resettlement. Beth wanted to bring him back to the house.

'I think you should leave him here,' I said. 'If we start having house pets, God knows where it will end.'

'He'll howl,' Beth said.

'Not for long. Put him in with whichever of the older bitches seems to take to him. She'll remind him of his mother. Just be sure she isn't coming into season.'

'You're a hard-hearted swine,' Beth said.

'If you say so.'

She grabbed my arm, pulled me down and kissed the side of my nose. 'Even if I say so, it isn't true. Under that abrasive manner, you're a soft touch. It's turning cold. Do you think Jason will be warm enough?'

'You wouldn't even ask the question if it were any other dog,' I said. 'He has a fur coat and he's used to a less luxurious kennel than that one.'

'I suppose so,' Beth said. 'But you don't have a fur coat. Come back to the house before you get chilled and I'll drink your health.'

'And Jason's I suppose?'

'Of course,' she said.

Henry had already got out my bottles. I couldn't grudge it to him after his weekend's efforts. His car was outside the door, but the Kitts' house was within a walkable distance. The meal was in front of us and the party was becoming quite jovial when I remembered something.

'That chap Bruce Fullerton,' I said. 'The one who came for his dog's portrait. Before her accident, his wife told him that she was going to have his dog put down. But I don't believe that anyone could have a perfectly healthy red setter destroyed.'

'That's because you couldn't do it,' Isobel said. 'There's hundreds who could.'

'Maybe you're right,' I admitted. 'But any vet would jib at destroying a perfectly healthy dog and I don't see her doing the job herself. Anyway, she might well hesitate if she was still hoping for a reconciliation. She may have put the dog into kennels, intending to give hubby a fright. They lived not far from here. If you hear over the kennels grapevine of somebody leaving a red setter for boarding, you might let me know.'

'It's a long shot,' Isobel said. 'The dog's probably been turned into atmospheric pollution by now. But I may be able to help. Mrs Whatshername at the boarding kennels rang up one evening, several weeks ago— '

'Mrs Spring,' Beth said.

'That's the woman. I can't imagine anyone being less vernal – which, I suppose, is why her name won't stay in my head. She wanted advice about a Jack Russell bitch infested with sheep ticks. They could have done the job themselves, but they're soft-hearted. I don't think that they can bring themselves to dab another living being with spirit and see it shrivel. I was delayed getting there – it was the Saturday Moonbeam went down with mastitis – and the Springs were in a hurry to go and meet their married daughter for a family celebration. The little bitch had ticks all over, including one on her eyelid – it wasn't a ten-minute job – so I promised to lock up when I'd finished and away they went. A little later, a very peculiar woman with one of those deep, sexy voices came to the door, wanting to board a red setter. She paid three months board in advance, showed a vaccination certificate and shot off. I don't suppose it's the same dog.'

'No more do I,' I said. 'But it could be. What name did she give?'

Isobel laid down her fork and stared into space for a minute. 'I don't remember,' she said. 'The dog's name was given as Rufus on the vaccination certificate.'

'I think that that's the name Fullerton mentioned,' I said. 'Of course, two male red setters out of three are named Rufus. But I'll give Fullerton a ring in the morning.'

Five

Monday morning, launchpad for another week.

With a whole regiment of spaniels, and now a Labrador, to claim my attention I still remembered one red setter separated from a caring owner. There were two B. Fullertons in the Fife and Kinross phonebook, but one of them lived a long way south in Burntisland. I phoned the other one early, to catch him before he left home. He recognised my voice immediately.

He took my news calmly and, I supposed, with a pinch of salt. I had my own doubts. That the missing dog should be found so easily seemed too good to be true. And yet, luck seemed to be running high. Perhaps it was time for some of it to rub off on somebody else.

We put in a hard morning's work but after lunch Isobel, who had lowered the level in the gin bottle the night before, suddenly jibbed at any more whistle-blowing or bangs from the dummy-launcher. Just as my remedy for the blues was to pick up a gun, hers was to do some gardening. The Kitts' garden was small and kept immaculate by Henry, so when the gardening urge came over Isobel she would usually launch an assault on the Three Oaks garden, much to Beth's disgust. As I set off towards The Moss with Gargany and Brockleton at heel and the Dickson over my arm, she had run out the electric cable and was reducing the hedge which separated the front garden from the next field to a shadow of its usual, shaggy self.

The big BMW met me at the gate, slowed and halted nearby. I left the two spaniels sitting and walked over.

The darkened, nearside window slid down, apparently of its own accord, and Fullerton leaned across. 'I came round to thank you,' he said. 'Your sources are good.' A red setter was curled on a blanket on a corner of the rear seat, watching us out of the corner of its eye and giving an occasional shiver.

'I'm glad,' I told him.

'I'm glad, too. You can't know what it means to have the old chap back. The house won't seem so empty now. He's still very nervous, but he'll get over it. If there's ever anything I can do in return— '

It seemed unlikely. But I was visited by a sudden curiosity. 'You could tell me what you were hiding when we met at Tarbet.'

'The reason I was surprised when I met Mrs Muir?' He thought it over for a few seconds. 'Well, why not. Get into the car.'

I glanced at the two spaniels. They were sitting tight, but a public roadside was not a good place to test their patience. 'Walk with me,' I suggested.

'Fine. Is it all right if I bring Rufus along?'

'I'd rather you didn't,' I said. The fewer distractions to dogs in training, the better; and the setter's nervous state might be communicated. 'If you don't mind.'

'No problem. After the favour you did me, your word is law. I'll pull forward to where I can park safely.'

He was safe where he was, but he drove forward and pulled off the road onto a section of hard verge beyond a clump of holly. He got out, turned to speak a few words to the setter and then locked up the car. A careful man, Bruce Fullerton, but not careful enough in his matrimonial life. When I caught up with him, we started walking. I had to adjust my stride to his shorter pace. The sun was shining half heartedly but a mist lay low over the land so that trees grew out of nothing and familiar walls and hedges appeared out of context.

'All right,' I said. 'What was so surprising about Harriet Muir?'

'I knew George Muir by sight,' he said, 'although I'd never met him. Then, several months ago, my wife and I went out to dinner at a small, country hotel – not a pretentious place, but they do you well and the wines aren't over-priced. I had a final brandy at the bar while she powdered her nose – my wife was doing the driving.' He sighed. 'I'll miss her as a driver on boozy evenings, if for not very much else. Anyway, I saw Muir registering at the hotel reception, with a plump, blonde woman. Naturally, I supposed that she was Mrs Muir. She went upstairs and Muir came into the bar so, on impulse, I spoke to him about a portrait of Rufus.

'Muir said that he'd need photographs to work from, but he'd also want the dog in his studio for an hour or two while he made preliminary sketches. I said that that would be easy enough, as I travel all over Scotland, but that I'd like to make it soon because I was going off to the States for some weeks. He looked in his diary and said to come two days later in the afternoon, which I did.

'His wife was out when I went there. In hindsight, I

suppose he'd guessed that I'd seen his companion and had chosen the day and time with that in mind. Yesterday, of course, I was expecting a chubby blonde. Meeting a dark and statuesque woman threw me for a moment, until I remembered hearing a whisper, some time ago, that he was a man for the ladies. Naturally, I didn't want to say anything while I was under her roof.'

'Naturally,' I said, wondering why not. 'Where was the hotel?' I asked.

He looked at me sharply. 'Why do you want to know that?'

'You just recommended it for a meal out,' I reminded him.

'That's true.' He told me the hotel's name. I already knew it and had found it disappointing.

He turned back shortly after that and I took the two spaniels on to The Moss. Gargany would need to be at the peak of training by the Saturday while, if Brockleton was bored with dummy work, some carrying and a few retrieves of the Real Thing would remind him of what it was all about.

So Beth's uncle had been a bit of a lad, and at his age! I remembered his face in the photograph. What I had taken to be a humorous twinkle in his eye might very well have been a lecherous gleam. When I thought about it, I had to admit to a sneaking sense of admiration. He had lived a life of infidelity until he was well past the age at which many men forget about sex altogether. And this he had contrived without ever being found out, as far as I knew, by his wife.

The mist was thinning to a faint haze. Brockleton pushed a rabbit out of a clump of reeds and I forgot all about George Muir.

* * *

Tuesday came in bright but cold, the best sort of winter's day. Frost had taken the moisture out of the air, hanging it instead as jewels on the branches. The sudden hills which are dotted around north-east Fife like the spots on a Dalmatian were so sharp that every blade of grass seemed to show, while the bare trees, usually a fuzz in the misty air, were sculptures of individual twigs.

Isobel arrived as I finished breakfast and we spent the morning putting the younger dogs through their paces on the grass. The dogs were skittish in the keen air so we kept it firm and simple. Beth finished the morning chores and came to help us. She was too proud to ask favours, but there was an expectant air about her, like a keen young dog waiting to be sent for a retrieve. I told her to go and get on with Jason's training. She grinned and we could soon see her at the far end of the grass, directing him with hand signals onto blind retrieves. Even Isobel seemed impressed.

After lunch, Isobel planned to take Gargany to The Moss. I intended to follow them up with the Dickson and give the two of them some practice in working to the gun, in preparation for Saturday's trial.

Isobel paused at the front door. 'I really must finish that hedge when I have a minute,' she said.

'I'll do it,' Beth said quickly.

'Would you?' Isobel said. 'It's an eyesore.'

Beth refrained from pointing out that the hedge was an eyesore not so much because of its half-trimmed state but because Isobel did not have a very straight eye. Its top had a sinuous line, like a grass snake or the parapet on one of Gaudi's buildings. 'Don't worry about it,' she said.

An hour later, I was ready to set out after Isobel.

But first, I felt the need of a hot drink. I went into the house and took off my heavy coat.

We had at last got round to fitting telephone extensions through the house. Beth was taking a call in the kitchen. On the stove, the percolator was bubbling as usual. Our comings and goings were often too irregular for the proper preparation of tea. I poured Beth a cup and put it by her elbow. She thanked me with a nod.

I was on the point of pouring a cup for myself when I heard a car on the gravel outside. Hoping for a customer, I went to the front door. A woman in her thirties, attractive in an Amazonian way, was getting out of a dusty saloon car. She had a haughty nose, a strong jaw and dark blonde hair which seemed to be held in perfect shape by strength of will rather than by any known lacquer. She was comfortably but smartly dressed for the cold weather, but I guessed that under the loose tweed coat there was a figure to set the hormones in motion. I was rather pleased with myself for the thought. It had been some years since I had felt unspecific lust.

'Mr Cunningham?'

I said that I was and asked what I could do with her. I meant to say 'for' her but my tongue made a Freudian slip.

She smiled a faint smile of superior amusement, as an aunt might smile at a child, but let it go by. 'Good morning, sir,' she said briskly. She produced a card. 'Sergeant Bedale. CID, Central Region. I want to discuss the death of George Muir. I believe you made some comments to the police in Tarbet.' She was crisp, no-nonsense and, I decided, probably the bossy type.

I looked round guiltily but nobody was in earshot

and most of the windows were closed against the cold of the day.

If Beth saw me alone with an attractive visitor we would never dislodge her, and I had no wish to share my doubts with any of George Muir's family unless and until I had to. For one thing, I still hoped that I might be making a stink for no good reason. So I ushered the sergeant into the sitting room. She seemed to march rather than walk. When I took her coat, I saw that the wool dress did indeed show off the sort of rounded figure which, while owing very little to artificial aids, would be an irritation to other women and a temptation to men. I tried not to admire it too obviously.

I indicated a chair. 'I was just going to have coffee,' I said. 'Will you join me?'

She nodded graciously. 'Black, no sugar.'

Beth was still on the phone. I poured two cups and carried them through. The sitting room was warm with the central heating, but its colours were cool and it always seemed bleak in winter with the fire laid but not lit. I put a match to the sticks and glanced for a moment at the blank wall above the mantel where George Muir's picture would hang. We settled down.

'I was expecting a reaction either much sooner or not at all,' I said.

'It went all the way to the top and came back down again,' she said. 'That took time. I'm told to look into it and to report whether it should be followed up further. You thought that it would be swept under the carpet?'

'I expected the local chap to drop it in the bin as soon as I was outside the door. I rather hoped that he would. That's probably what I'd have done myself, in his place. I certainly made it clear that I had no intention of taking it any further. Having doubts, I felt I had to report them. But I could still hope that I was wrong.'

'That's understandable.' She looked at me, considering. 'What you expected might well have happened. But I think that the officers who went to investigate may have been a bit high-handed with the local men.' She opened a capacious leather handbag and flipped a large notebook out and open in a single movement. 'Tell me about cartridge loading. Why do men load their own. To save money?'

'Not entirely. The commonest shotgun is the twelve-bore and the mainstream twelve-bore cartridge is churned out by the million. If you buy in quantity you can buy good cartridges almost as cheaply as you can load them yourself. But I suppose the makers have to stop the production line to put other cartridges through, so you pay just as much for smaller cartridges. And the magnum cartridges cost the earth.'

'Magnum cartridges, such as Mr Muir was loading, would be necessary for geese?' she asked.

'Arguably yes,' I said. 'It's a matter of preference. Geese are big and they fly high. According to the pundits, you use your fieldcraft to be where you'll have them within range, but that's easier written than done. There's a lot to be said for giving yourself a margin of range. It can make the difference between a clean kill and a pricked bird. The other reason for loading your own is that you can't always buy the cartridge you want when you want it. But you can find a loading recipe which gives you exactly what you want and stick to it.'

She was jotting rapidly in shorthand as I spoke.

'And how is this piece of magic performed?' she asked.

'You can get a machine, but if you don't load many cartridges it could take a lifetime to pay for itself. George Muir used hand-tools. Hang on and I'll show you. I used to hand-load. I don't keep the materials any more – the business buys me my cartridges – but I still have the tools.'

I went through the kitchen. In my little workshop and junk room behind the 'shop' I got out my old hand-tools and a spent cartridge. I opened the gun-safe and dropped a live cartridge into my pocket.

On the way back I noticed that Beth, who was still on the phone, had finished her coffee. I removed the cup and laid a knife and fork in front of her. 'Very funny,' she said. She returned to the phone. 'No, I was speaking to John. He's being sarcastic. Go on.'

I kissed the top of her head and went on through to the drawing room. 'Here are my own tools,' I said. 'George Muir's were similar, except that his is a beautiful antique set with ivory handles and adjustable measures.

'Here's a fired cartridge case and here's an unfired one.' I put the two plastic cases in front of her. 'The first step is to re-size the cases – using this— ' I showed her the re-sizing die. 'And something has to make the thing go bang when the firing pin hits it, so you have to replace the primer.' I went through an outline of the motions.

'George Muir had already re-sized and primed his empty cases. It's easier to do one step at a time with all of them. You build up a rhythm and you aren't constantly switching tools.

'His next step would have been to put powder into

the cases, using a measure like this one, and push a wad down on top. He used fibre wads - miniature cylinders, rather than the moulded plastic wads. And the final step— '

'You needn't go on,' she said. 'I load for my husband, so I do know the basics of reloading. I just wanted to know how much you knew about it. Now tell me why you're so sure that it wasn't an accident.'

I felt myself flush. Perhaps I had been using a patronising tone borrowed from children's television. But she had led me to believe that she was starting from scratch. There had been no need for such a set-down. I decided that I did not like Sergeant Bedale. But, I reminded myself, I had invoked the police and she was their representative. I did not have to like her.

'Have you been to the studio?' I asked.

'Not yet. There would have been no point until I knew what you were suggesting.' Something in her tone as well as in her choice of words let me know that my suggestions were of only faint interest and probably indecent.

I held onto my temper. 'I don't know that I'm suggesting anything in particular,' I said. 'I noticed some anomalies and I'm passing them on. George Muir had two iron pots on the work-bench in his studio, one for powder and one for shot. They seem to have been small cooking pots, but they were ideal for his purpose – wide enough to get a hand into while holding a spoon or a measure, and with tight-fitting lids which couldn't easily be dislodged. His powder would be perfectly safe in a pot like that while the lid was firmly on. You follow me?'

She nodded without looking up from her notes.

'The pot which had held his powder had been pulled forward to the middle of the bench. There was a tiny hole in it.'

That made her look up. 'There was nothing in the original report about a hole.'

'It was very inconspicuous. A very small hole in a black pot all stained with soot, seen against the shadow on the bench beyond it.'

Her eyes – which, I noticed, were a surprisingly dark blue – were fastened on me, but as if I had been a fingerprint or a bloodstain rather than a living, breathing person. 'How did it happen that you noticed what a trained detective had missed?'

'I only spotted the hole because I happened to seat myself so that I was looking through it to where the light was falling on the pale bench beyond. Even so, it took me some time to realise that it was a hole and not a fleck of something pale. But if the hole had been there for any length of time, Muir would have noticed it. He'd have been bound to see grains of spilled powder on the bench – it becomes a habit to look for them and sweep them up. He could easily have changed over and put the shot into the pot with the hole in it – the hole was much too small to pass the Number Three shot which he was using. So the hole must have been new and he didn't know that it was there.'

Sergeant Bedale looked up again. 'The explosion could have found a flaw in the metal. A piece of included slag.'

The fire had burned up and was casting a flattering glow on her. Her face now looked as if it might sometimes be friendly, but I was not going to respond to it. She had been playing me along. Although I was doing most of the talking, she still had control. The one thing guaranteed to light my fuse was any reference to 'the public', suggesting that the speaker was somehow poised above an amorphous and commonplace herd. Even while I was in the army I had seen the ranks of supposedly regimented and identical soldiers and had known that they were individuals, each with his virtues and his aspirations; but the police, I knew, often fell into the trap of this 'them and us' attitude. The Sergeant, treating me as a member of 'the public' and therefore of an inferior order, made me itch to smack her bottom.

It took an effort of will to remain calm and polite. 'It's within the bounds of possibility,' I said, 'although the hole looked too neat and round for that. But next, how did a spark arrive at the powder? His wife was adamant that he had knocked his pipe out before going through and that the explosion occurred only a few seconds later. I can't accept the idea of a spark strong enough to last the journey that was neither felt nor smelled.

'Either the lid was still on the pot or it wasn't. If the lid was off, the powder would have burned rather than exploded. Shotgun propellant is normally a comparatively slow-burning explosive. It has to be confined if it's going to build up pressure for an explosion. The lid of the other pot fitted tightly. It took quite an effort to remove it. That would have provided enough resistance. What's more, the lid must have been in place from the way it had fragmented and the bits of it were sent flying around the room. So whatever triggered the explosion was an internal mechanism or it was introduced through that small hole.

'Finally, Sergeant, there had been shot pellets in with the powder. It had added to the shrapnel effect. No home-loader would ever allow that to happen.

Sooner or later, he'd fire a shot while some pellets from the previous cartridge were still in the barrel. He'd end up with little bulges like pimples along the expensive barrel of his gun.'

I ground to a halt at last.

Sergeant Bedale put down her notebook and finished her coffee. She stared into the fire. I waited patiently. 'You were quite right to bring this to our attention,' she said. A pat on the head for a good boy. 'It'll have to be looked into. But, just off the top of my head, I can see other explanations for what you've told me – always assuming that your observations were accurate.

'Consider this possibility. George Muir knew about the small hole in the pot, so he did as you suggested. He used that pot for his shot. On the occasion when he finished sizing and priming his empty cases, he decided to top up his pots ready for the next step in his reloading programme. It happened that the powder pot was empty, but there was still some shot in the other. By mistake he switched the pots over and decanted powder on top of the shot.

'Then, on the evening of his death, he went through to the studio. He pulled forward the container which now held powder along with some shot. In the process some powder escaped onto the bench. At the last moment, he decided to do something else before beginning to reload – cleaning the tools or checking his measures perhaps. So he had time for another pipe. Or perhaps whatever he decided to do entailed a flame or the production of sparks from his grindstone. The powder on the bench ignited and . . . boom! After such a disturbance in the room, the signs of what he was doing might well be confused or even destroyed.'

It was my turn to look into the flames. Her theory was ingenious and just as probable as my own. But there was something wrong. It took me a few seconds to remember.

'There was very little sign of charring on the bench,' I said. 'It's built of white wood, slightly grubby but unvarnished. There would have been random burns on the surface. But the only burn mark on it was a faint, straight line. That was what led my eye to the hole in the first place. It could have been made by the escaping flash from the explosion.'

'But?' she said. The damned woman could read either my tone or my mind.

'But it did make me wonder, for a moment, about the possibility of a fuse.'

'A burning fuse would have left a distinct but irregular burn mark,' she said.

'Perhaps. I was thinking about a fuse made from a pipe-cleaner, one of those woolly wire things. The first fuses were made by soaking a piece of rope in a solution of saltpetre and . . . ' for the moment, memory failed me, ' . . . and something else. You could do that to a pipe-cleaner. The wire would have entered the hole neatly and the pipe-cleaner would have stuck out horizontally just above the surface of the bench. It would probably be blown against the wall by the explosion and have fallen down the back of the bench. Who'd think anything about a burned pipe-cleaner among the mess?'

She went back to her scribbling, but she must have been able to write shorthand and think logically at the same time. 'A delayed action which caught him just as he arrived at the bench,' she said. 'Not easily judged.'

That had been my own first thought. 'He could

have been drugged or knocked on the head,' I pointed out. 'Then the delay would only have been necessary in order to give his murderer time to get out of the room.'

'That would seem to rule out any outsiders. You seem to be suggesting that George Muir was murdered by his wife.'

I opened my mouth to deny it, but we were interrupted.

'Oh my God!' Beth's voice said from the door. 'Oh my God! John, what have you done?'

I turned my head so quickly that I nearly ricked my neck. Beth was standing in the doorway, white-faced. I got up quickly and went to her. I held out my hands, but she hid hers behind her back.

Sergeant Bedale's head was lowered tactfully over her notebook.

'How could you?' Beth asked.

'Please,' I said, 'don't work up a head of steam until I've told you about it.' Beth's eyes were wandering, unseeing, around the room. 'Listen to me,' I said. 'I honestly don't think I've done anything that you wouldn't have wanted me to do, or that you wouldn't have done yourself if our positions had been reversed. I came across certain signs that your uncle's death might not have been accidental. Would you expect me to stay dumb and let it be passed off as an accident?'

'You could have told me,' she said in a small voice.

'I suppose I could. But what was the point of upsetting you and Hattie when I wasn't sure of anything? If you'd found something to suggest that your uncle was probably murdered, would you have kept quiet about it?' I persisted.

'Well, no. But I'd have consulted you before rushing off to the police.'

'I didn't want to worry you. I hope – I still hope – that there's nothing in it. This is Sergeant Bedale. She's come over to follow it up. I don't think that she agrees with me. So that's probably an end to the matter. This is Beth,' I told the Sergeant. 'My fiancée and George Muir's niece.'

'How do you do?' Beth said politely and then turned back to me. 'But you said that Hattie killed him.'

'I said nothing of the sort. Sit down, calm down and listen for another moment.' I persuaded her to join me on the couch although she perched at the far end like a nervous sparrow. 'The Sergeant inferred that I was putting the blame on Hattie – the widow,' I explained to Sergeant Bedale. 'Harriet Muir. But I wasn't, Beth. The Muirs seem to have been very careless about keys, leaving the front-door key above the door. I wondered about Hattie at first, but I couldn't see such a houseproud woman letting off a bomb in her own house. And the unsold paintings in the studio represented a large capital sum for her to inherit. She wouldn't have destroyed them.'

The Sergeant waited. When Beth made no comment, she said dispassionately, 'That might depend on how pressing her motivation was.'

'They were fond of each other,' Beth said. 'Not stormy lovers but quietly fond.' Her eyes filled with tears. I held out my handkerchief but she ignored it.

Such subjective comment was beneath the Sergeant's notice. 'Are you sure that you want to stay here?' she asked kindly. 'You may find the rest of what we have to say distressing.'

Beth nodded decisively.

'Very well.' Sergeant Bedale waited until she had made eye contact with me and then resurrected our discussion. 'You suggested a delayed action device. It's possible. A burning fuse would leave a smell in the air which Mr Muir would certainly have noticed if he had been conscious.'

'Almost certainly,' I said. 'Although he'd just finished smoking a pipe.'

'True. Or there could have been an electrical timer. There was plenty of time for somebody to remove it before anybody else arrived. But that brings us back to the wife again. Who else could get into the house, set up a timer, perhaps knock Mr Muir on the head and remove the evidence after the explosion without Mrs Muir at least being aware of their presence?'

Beth was looking stunned at this dispassionate discussion of her uncle's death. 'But that's not how you'd do such a thing,' she protested.

'If that's how it was done,' I said, 'I share your doubts. But the objective may have been something quite different. It could be that George Muir was unlucky. Perhaps what was intended was an act of vandalism or spite resulting in the destruction of the paintings. Or a fire to wipe out all the contents of the studio. An explosion doesn't often result in a fire, but whoever rigged it might not know that. It may have been the purest bad luck that George Muir arrived at his bench as it went off.'

The Sergeant had closed her notebook. She drummed her fingernails on the cover, making a sound like hoofbeats. 'We're getting away from facts into the wildest speculation,' she said, 'but I can't see any reason for somebody to want to burn out a studio, except possibly for the insurance. And guess who that would bring us back to!'

'I don't suppose that the paintings were insured for more than a tenth of their sale value,' I said. 'Many of the pictures were of shooting scenes. Muir portrayed shooting in its real colours, as an honest and legitimate outdoor recreation, not as the sadistic and bloodthirsty activity its opponents would have you believe in. He showed gundogs at work as being happy and fulfilled. You could say that he was a very credible publicist for fieldsports. People like the League Against Cruel Sports and the Hunt Saboteurs might well resent his work.'

Beth had got up to put another log on the fire. She turned and faced us. 'There could have been a reason why somebody wanted the studio to burn,' she said. 'I don't say that there was, but it's possible. And I'm not saying what it might have been, so don't ask me. Please.'

'I won't,' I said. 'Come back here before you set your bum on fire.'

She moved away from the flames and patted her backside absently. She managed to look simultaneously both angry and reluctantly amused. 'I'll set yours alight if you've started something awful,' she said gloomily. 'That was Hattie on the phone. She sounded miserable. She's coming over here to stay with us for a few days.'

The Sergeant got to her feet. 'Call her back quickly,' she snapped. 'Ask her to leave her key with the local police. Say that the procurator fiscal has asked for a few more details about the damage before he closes the file.'

Beth looked sullen. I was not the only one to resent the Sergeant's authoritative manner. 'You call her,' she said. 'I'm not telling her any lies. If I call her, I'll tell her the truth.' She looked at me. The hurt in her eyes was still there but now she was asking for support. 'Juliet Bravo here can't make me tell lies for her, can she?'

'I think that it would be kindest to leave Hattie in the dark until we're sure, one way or the other,' I said. 'If this is upsetting for you, imagine how it would be for her.'

Beth considered. My reasoning overcame her desire to be stubborn. 'All right, then!' She slammed out of the room.

'You do seem to be headed for the doghouse,' the Sergeant said cheerfully. 'No pun intended. How certain are you that the hole wasn't drilled in the pot after the explosion?' When I stared at her stupidly, she went on, 'There is one other possibility to consider. George Muir blew himself up accidentally and now somebody is trying to make it look like murder.'

'Do you mean me?' I asked.

She smiled at me, but there was no warmth in it. 'Does the cap fit? If Mr Muir was murdered by his wife, the law would debar her from inheriting his estate. Who do you suppose would be next in line?'

'I haven't the faintest idea,' I said. 'I know that George Muir left a will. Ask the lawyers.'

Beth came back into the room. 'And just what am I supposed to say to Hattie if she asks how I know what the procurator fiscal wants?' she asked.

The Sergeant laughed without looking abashed and went out with her.

While the Sergeant made her phone call, I decided to keep my head down and to stay out of the way. I loaded various bags and the feeding dishes onto a shopping trolley and trundled out to the kennels.

The evening feed was a complex business. One

dog needed building up, the next tended to put on weight, while yet another had had jaundice as a pup and was kept off fats. A diet, agreed jointly by the three of us, was written in Magic Marker on a piece of white plastic at the gate to each run. But dogs were sometimes shifted around and it took concentration, in the teeth of canine impatience which was soon mounting to frenzy, to be sure that each dog was getting the right diet.

After ten minutes, the Sergeant came out of the house, gave me an impersonal wave and drove away. Beth brought out a basin of warm mush for the young puppies.

She was thoughtful and in no mood for chatter, which suited me. I felt that I had said more than enough already. But when the dishes had been carried back to the house and washed, she jerked her head at me. 'You've lit the fire,' she said. 'It seems a pity to waste it. So we may as well talk in the sitting room.'

I followed her through. I could tell from her walk that she was winding herself up for an explosion. But when she had built up the fire again she seated herself, well away from me, and said, almost mildly, 'You'd better tell me all about it.'

'All right,' I said.

'And don't take too long. I'll have to go and prepare the spare room. Hattie can move in with me.'

If I was being banished to the small spare room, things were really bad between us. Least said, soonest mended, I told myself and then remembered that it was that philosophy that had laid the foundation for our present troubles. If I had taken Beth into my confidence from the first she would not be so hurt and angry now. With a little luck she might even have talked me out of my suspicions.

I had hardly begun my explanation when there was a knock. The door partly opened and Henry's colourful features appeared, as always surprisingly high up. One tended to forget how tall Henry was.

'Thought I might find somebody in here,' he said amiably. 'I walked over to see whether Isobel was ready to come home. Stopped at the hotel for a beer or two on the way,' he added superfluously. Henry's capacity for beer was phenomenal. He seemed to sense tension in the air. 'If this is a private fight, I'll go away.'

'You'd better come in, Henry,' Beth said tiredly. 'The world and his wife will know all about it soon enough, since John decided to shoot his mouth off.'

'Only to the police.' I said. 'You're the one who's broadcasting it.'

She ignored me. 'You may even be able to make a useful comment,' she added. 'It's time that somebody made one.'

Henry raised his shaggy eyebrows and came all the way in. 'At least I can hold your coats,' he said. He folded himself down onto the settee.

They listened intently while I told the story. In deference to Beth's feelings, I left out any mention of her uncle's womanising, but I covered the rest in detail. Henry asked a few technical questions, but Beth was more interested in the theories which the Sergeant and I had offered to each other.

When I came to a lame halt, Beth looked at Henry. 'What do you think?'

Henry took his time answering. 'I don't know whether your uncle met his end by fair means or foul,' he said, 'but there does seem to be cause for a more positive investigation. In John's place, I think I'd have done exactly as he did – if I'd been astute enough to see the flaws in the accident theory. Be fair, young Beth. He couldn't just leave things alone, as long as there was the possibility that a murderer was walking free. And there was no point in creating tension between yourselves and Mrs Muir. The whole thing might have been discounted or have blown over.'

That took the wind out of Beth's sails. 'Oh,' she said.

'Seems to me,' Henry said, 'that John's held his tongue remarkably well, until you made him let go of it.'

Beth was not going to let me off without having the last word. 'He'd better go on guarding his tongue while Hattie's here,' she said. 'She's coming to visit.'

'You both had,' Henry said. 'God knows what reaction a careless word might provoke. I don't want to put wrong ideas into your minds, but doesn't it occur to you that you may, just possibly, be welcoming a murderess into your home?'

'Oh,' Beth said again. For a moment, she looked almost her real age. 'No, I don't believe it. I can't. What do we say if she mentions her phone-call from that sergeant woman?'

'As little as possible,' I said.

The room went quiet except for the crackle of the dying fire.

'I've got work to do,' Beth said suddenly. She got to her feet and marched out of the room.

'I owe you a drink,' I told Henry. I was in dire need of one myself. 'Then I'd better go to The Moss and tell Isobel I'm not coming.'

Henry waited until he had a drink safely in his hand before he spoke again. 'Don't celebrate too soon,' he said. 'At the moment, Beth's wondering whether she's been the victim of a male conspiracy.'

'You're wrong,' I said. 'She's wondering whether she'd rather share a bedroom with a possible murderess or a definite trouble-maker.'

Six

It was late evening before Hattie arrived, in George Muir's large estate car. 'It will have to go,' were her first words. 'George needed the size of it to carry his paints and canvases in the back, but it fairly gobbles up the petrol. That may not have mattered to George when he was making money out of it and running it before tax, but I'm a widow woman now.'

'Before you offer it to Alistair Young,' I said, 'give me a chance to top his offer.' I was joking, but my old estate car had seen a lot of miles in its time.

Hattie gave a snort of laughter. She had had a meal, she said, but yes, she would be glad of tea . . . coffee . . . chocolate . . . anything warm and wet.

I looked at the big car and wondered what other uses George Muir might have had for the back of it.

Old Mona descended stiffly from the car and looked at her new surroundings without any great interest. She also had been fed, Hattie told us, and her inoculation certificates were up to date. I took her out to the kennels and left her to share a run and kennel with Jason, the only one of our dogs she had met before. After a little preliminary sniffing they settled down cheerfully together.

Beth and Hattie were sipping hot chocolate at the table in the kitchen. Hattie looked at home in the cluttered, all-purpose room. 'Where are your cases?' I asked her.

'Beth fetched them upstairs.' She took a look at me in the light and turned to Beth. 'He's looking washed out. Are you letting him overwork? Or is he worried about something?'

'He's a born worrier,' Beth said lightly, but she stole an anxious glance at me.

'You don't mind me foisting myself on you like this?' Hattie asked me. 'After all, it's your house and I'm not even a blood relative to Beth.'

I laid my hand on her shoulder and sensed nothing but goodwill through the contact. Surely if she had had murder on her conscience I would have felt it? 'After all your generosity?' I said. 'Don't be silly.'

'It was nothing. If I made you happy, I'm glad. And to arrive so late in the night,' she added. 'I was almost ready to leave when I had a call from the police, asking me to leave the key at the local police station.'

Beth jumped and opened her mouth, preparatory to putting her foot in it. 'Just as well,' I said quickly. 'Are you always so trusting with keys, leaving them on the ledge above the door?'

Hattie shrugged. 'Why not? We've never been burgled. It's so that Grant Nolan and my daily woman can let themselves in.'

The name rang a distant bell in my mind. 'Do you trust Grant Nolan?' I asked.

'I trust him to keep the garden and to do odd jobs around the place. I'd not want to let him away with a key, likely he'd drop it in the first pub he came to.'

'But Hattie,' I said, 'he could just as easily tell

everybody in the pub that the key's over the door.'

'When he's been drinking,' Hattie said firmly, 'he wouldn't remember that there was a door, let alone a key to it. But he's a good worker when he's sober or near it. I had him give me a hand this afternoon. The police want to take one last look at the place before the fiscal closes the file. Well, I couldn't have them seeing it the way it was so we spent a whilie in clearing up.'

I tried not to look horrified. 'In the studio?' I said.

'Aye. The rest of the house was tidy. Yon mannie from Glasgow whose card you gave me, the picture mender with the funny name . . . '

'Mr Grogan.'

'Aye, him. He'd been there earlier in the day and he'd uplifted all of the pictures and sketches to sort through. He's going to give me a price for mending them and another for frames. It'll cost a fine penny to sort them, so he said, but worth it in the end because otherwise I'd be paying the agent's commission on top. He says that most of the sketches are worth putting on the market, in dribs and drabs.'

'But the studio— ' Beth said in a choked voice.

'The studio was already more than half empty, with the pictures gone. It only needed a clear-out and a good clean.' Beth and I were both dumbstruck. Hattie misinterpreted our silence. 'That was the first time I'd been in there since the night George died. It didn't bother me the way I'd thought it would. It was just another room.'

Beth met my eye for a moment. Was Hattie being innocent or brazen? I was damned if I could tell. Beth had something else on her mind.

'Excuse me a moment,' she said. 'I'll be right

back.' She scuttled out and I could hear her banging around upstairs.

'There's a carton in your hall,' Hattie said to me. 'I thought that since you have George's gun you may as well have the rest of his shooting gear. It's only an old belt and some cartridges and his loading things. I'm letting his clothes go to charity and Grant Nolan can have his tools. I'll not be taking up woodwork at my time of life.'

'But Hattie,' I said, 'those loading tools are antiques. I'm sure they're valuable.'

As Beth came back and slumped into her chair, Hattie leaned across and patted my hand. 'Don't fash yourself,' she said. 'You did me a good turn when you told me that Alistair Young was trying to – what was it you said? – to "rip me off". I asked around, and I found that the surveyor he wanted us to get to price the difference between our houses is an old, old crony of his. I got a man of my own to come by yesterday and the figures are very different. Alistair's dancing mad,' she added with satisfaction.

'You're still going through with the exchange?' Beth asked.

'Oh aye. I'll like their wee house fine if I have that wee bittie extra to spend on it. But the Youngs will have to come up with a bigger mortgage than they were planning on. Alistair's been on at me all day. And Edgar came by just before the Grogan mannie, to choose his picture. He went off with a big painting of the view across the loch to Ben Lomond.'

I could have bet on it. Edgar had chosen the largest and least damaged painting, the one most likely to turn a profit.

'He was calling you all the names under the sun,'

Hattie said. 'Told me you'd gone off with the wrong dog. He says he'll sue you.'

'He won't, will he?' Beth said anxiously.

'Not a chance,' I said. 'You'll note that he hasn't phoned us here. Isobel's prepared to swear that Jason – our Jason – is a direct descendant of Farthingale Bonus, while nobody could mistake that other beast for one of that line. Add my threat to have them genetically fingerprinted and to leave him stuck with the cost . . . No, he won't sue.'

'Likely not,' Hattie said. 'But with them all coming at me, I was just scunnered. I decided I'd best up sticks and get away for a few days. I'm no great hand with dogs, but I can make myself useful.'

'You just take it easy and rest up,' I told her.

'They say that a change is as good as a rest,' Hattie said. 'I feel the need of a change, but I couldn't be doing with idleness. Is that the time? And you two will be early risers with all those dogs to look after. It's high time I was away to my bed and let you get to yours.'

'You're in the small room on the left at the head of the stairs,' Beth said. 'The bathroom's next door to you.'

I tried not to look pleased and surprised. It seemed that I was back in favour. When Hattie's footsteps had climbed the stairs I said, 'Have you decided that you couldn't live without me?'

Beth came round the table and perched on my knee. It could not have been a very comfortable knee, with so little flesh over the bones, but she was very light. 'When she said that you looked tired and worried, I realised that what you'd done hadn't been easy.' Beth lowered her voice to a whisper. 'And there was another thing.'

'What?' I whispered back.

'She's made quite a job of scattering all the evidence. It could have been innocently done. But I remembered what Henry said. I don't know that I believe it, but I'm not sure that I don't. It's something like not walking under a ladder, or under a tree when there's a gale blowing. I just didn't fancy sharing a room with somebody who might be a murderess.'

'Henry doesn't miss much,' I said.

When we were in bed and I was on the point of dropping off, I was jerked into wakefulness by a sudden recollection. Beth was still reading. I rolled over and looked at her – never anything but a pleasure even when she had cream all over her face and reading glasses on her small nose.

'You said that somebody might have wanted to burn the studio,' I said softly. 'What was it you wouldn't tell the Sergeant or Henry?'

'I suppose there's no harm telling you. But this is for your ears only.' She closed her book on a marker and laid it aside. 'Can you keep a secret?'

'You know damn well— ' I began.

She shushed me and pointed at the door.

The house was solidly built and the doors fitted well, but I lowered my voice anyway. 'You know damn well I can,' I said.

'And you won't be funny about it?'

'I don't suppose so.'

She put her book down and turned to face me. 'Well . . . Uncle George was an awful man for the women.'

I felt myself jump. 'I knew that. I didn't know that you did.'

'I've known for years. How did you find out?'

'Bruce Fullerton told me. He'd seen him with a chubby blonde once. That's why he seemed surprised when he met Hattie.'

'Uncle George thought that he was being very clever and careful,' Beth said, 'but I knew even when I was at school. All the girls at school with me knew that he was my uncle, and whenever one of them saw him with another lady they'd tell me – not to score off me but as something to giggle about. He had a fatherly sort of charm which seemed to make them want to roll over and have their tummies tickled. Not the schoolgirls – we were too young to see him as anything but an old man. But I think that some of their mothers and aunts used to think of Uncle George when they were making love with their husbands.'

'It came over in that photograph of him,' I said.

'I bet a woman took that photograph,' Beth said thoughtfully. She made one of her sudden and confusing changes of subject. 'Did you know that there's a gallery in Italy which has a whole wing devoted to the paintings that great artists have knocked off for the erotic amusement of themselves or their best clients? The public doesn't get to go inside, it's kept for VIPs. Typical!' Beth murmured sleepily.

'Do they have any George Muirs hanging there?'

Beth elbowed me. 'You promised you wouldn't make any jokes!'

'It was a serious question. I'll ask a different one. Did your uncle do that sort of thing?' I asked.

'I don't know that he did it often,' Beth said. 'But, as he got older, he may have needed a turn-on. When you went into the studio with Mr Fullerton, did you go through all his sketches?'

'No. As far as I remember, Fullerton found what

he wanted near the top of the pile. I think he glanced through the rest of them, but we were talking about something else at the time.'

Beth snuggled up against me. Her voice was barely audible even at that small distance. Her breath tickled my chin. 'You remember that I took a week's holiday last spring? I went through by train and Uncle George picked me up from Dumbarton.

'He used to let me come and sit with him in the studio while he painted, because I could sit quietly. I think that I was the only person he ever allowed inside the door. Hattie was forbidden the place. He said that she fidgeted and moved things around. Anyway, he used to get totally absorbed in his painting. I enjoyed watching him and seeing the painting grow under his brush.

'Once, to while away the time, I glanced through the pile of sketches. And very good most of them were too. He looked round suddenly, saw what I was doing and told me to come away from there, quite sharply. But not before I'd seen one in particular. It was a finished drawing rather than a sketch. It was so good that I thought for a moment it was a photograph.'

'A nude?' I asked.

'It was a bit more than that. Sort of soft porn. Nothing perverse, but it was – what's the word I want? – lascivious, I think. Every fetish in the book and some I'd never heard of. It made me feel hot, and I'm not even a man.'

'Was it anybody you knew?' I asked.

'No. But I'd know her again anywhere. And if there was a lot of that sort of material around somebody might easily want to bomb the place.'

'Or even kill two Uncle Georges with one stone,' I said. 'I wonder what Grogan will make of them.'

'Mr Grogan said that he could be very discreet,' Beth reminded me. 'I think that's what he meant. So Uncle George's habit of putting his randiest fantasies – if they were fantasies – down on paper couldn't have been that much of a secret. Maybe some of them have found their way onto the black market before now. Or else he knew that all artists leave that sort of legacy behind. Anyway, Grogan didn't get them. I sneaked into the studio and went through the pile on Sunday morning while you were still having breakfast. There was nothing I couldn't have shown the minister in the presence of all the elders of the kirk and their mothers.'

I tried to visualise such a drawing and failed. Another thought came to me. 'A drawing like that would hardly be proof of anything. I mean, a competent artist could draw a body and put anybody's face on it. For all you know, there's an erotic drawing somewhere with your head on its shoulders.'

'Do you think so?' Beth said. She snorted with laughter so that her soft shape jiggled against me. 'So if one turns up, you'll believe me when I tell you that I didn't pose for it?'

'Who's making jokes now?' I said. I found the thought distressful. 'Well, we'll cross that bridge if we ever come to it. I suppose your uncle was above blackmail? Think how easy it would be for him to paint a study of some prominent lady, wearing nothing but lace pants and a come hither smile, and threaten to put it in his next show. Most of them would buy it for a fancy price just to keep it out of circulation.' I stopped to think about it and an immediate snag occurred to me. 'But if he was getting fancy prices for his work anyway, he wouldn't have needed to risk being sued or murdered, would he?'

Beth said nothing. All the talk about erotic paintings had begun to put me in a certain mood but I realised suddenly that she had fallen asleep.

Henry, of course, had told the whole story to Isobel, who arrived next morning in a mood in which curiosity and suspicion were nicely mingled.

Hattie, as she had admitted, was no hand with dogs; but she was a willing worker, had a sturdy Highland physique and did not turn up her nose at such tasks as clearing dogs' messes from the grass. She could also throw a dummy further than any of us. Isobel soon forgot, or had never accepted, that Hattie was suspect. The two older ladies became as thick as thieves.

It was hardly to be expected that Sergeant Bedale would leave us in peace. She turned up, late on the Wednesday morning, very neat in grey flannel, while I was teaching a small group of youngsters on the grass. Her air of being in command had diminished and she was even conciliatory to the point of patting any dog who came within reach. Hattie and Isobel had gone off to The Moss together and Beth was out in the car, fetching supplies of biscuit meal. I kennelled the dogs and took the Sergeant through the shop into my junk room.

'I saw the burn mark on the work-bench,' she said. 'You were right – it looks too tidy to be the result of spillage. And that was all that I managed to see,' she added, more in sorrow than anger. 'Everything else, *every* other damn thing, had been tidied away, carried off or swept up. Sometimes I wonder how the human race has managed to make even such little progress as it has, with every second member of it too stupid to come in out of the rain.'

'Well, don't rage me about it,' I said. 'I didn't do it and it wasn't my idea. Presumably you've collected the contents of her dustbin?'

The Sergeant, who was in a fractious mood, threw up her eyes. 'I have. And somewhere among the cabbage stalks and rotten tomatoes there may be some tiny item like your burned pipe-cleaner. And I was told not to go for any help from Forensic until after my report's been considered and accepted. It's a lovely life!'

'Let me bring a little sunshine into it. Mrs Muir brought me her husband's shooting and reloading gear, so you may find some of what you want in this lot.'

I lifted the heavy carton onto my own work-bench and opened it. The two pots and a bag of shot accounted for most of the weight.

'Shall I leave you to it?' I asked.

'You stay.' She meant it for a command but it came out as a request. Adversity had humanised the Sergeant. 'You've sown the wind which brought me this impossible and thankless job. If somebody has to reap the whirlwind, you're elected. Where's this celebrated hole?'

I could easily have told her to do her own snooping but, in truth, I was becoming interested. I lifted out the lidless pot and rotated it until I could point out the hole. She studied it from all angles, including lifting it to look through it at the light.

'It's round,' she said at last. 'Perfectly round. It was drilled. And it's sooty. What size is it?'

I got out my set of twist drills. She took them from me and probed gently. 'I don't want the soot disturbed more than necessary,' she said. She satisfied herself that a drill of 1/16 inch diameter seemed to fit exactly, made a note in her ever-present book and peered gloomily into the bottom of the pot. 'I suppose we have to be thankful that it hasn't been scoured out with a Brillo pad,' she said. 'Without destroying any evidence, what do you make of this guck in the bottom?'

'Mostly burned powder,' I said. 'You must know what that looks like as well as I do, if you've been helping your husband. I thought that it seemed to be mixed with the ash of paper plus a few pellets of shot.'

We stood, peering into the pot like two of the witches in *Macbeth*. The Sergeant poked the sooty bottom with the blunt end of her ballpoint. 'There's a little lump of something stuck there,' she said.

'Probably melted pellets among the burned powder,' I said. 'You'd better save it for the lads from Forensic, if it ever gets that far.'

'If.' She tore a page out of her notebook, laid it on my work-bench and tipped the pot over it. A few grains of powder drifted down onto the white paper. 'It doesn't look quite right,' she said. 'When we push a wad of paper through my husband's gun, as a first step towards cleaning it, the soot looks very much like this but not quite the same.'

'Well it wouldn't,' I said.

Her dark blue eyes shot a suspicious look right through me. 'Why not?'

'I wouldn't expect it to be the same powder. What does your husband use?'

'Nobel Eighty,' she said.

'For geese . . . ' I looked deep in the carton and found the white tin which I had seen in the drawer in the studio. It was cross hatched with blue and pink lines. From the weight, it was nearly full. 'I thought so,' I said. 'French *Poudre T*. A large-grained, progressive powder, more suited to magnum loads. Unburnt, it's a silvery colour, quite unlike the usual black or dark grey.'

The Sergeant had a habit of not seeming to listen, although I was sure that she would be able to quote my words against me if the occasion should arise. She had taken the tin from me and was weighing it in her hands. After a careful look around, in case some naked light should be waiting to pounce, she unscrewed the lid and peered inside. 'Silver,' she said. 'And nearly full.'

I rooted again in the carton and found a few spent magnum shells, presumably cartridges which George Muir had fired since he began the reloading process on the rest, but they were internally clean. A cartridge is in the area of greatest pressure and combustion is usually complete. I tipped a little of the silver powder into the lid of a tin and struck a match. The Sergeant retired as far as the confines of the room would allow. The powder flared spectacularly but harmlessly. I tipped the remaining burnt grains onto another page.

The Sergeant peered at the tiny grains. 'Similar,' she said at last. 'I think, without being sure, that there's a difference in colour. I'm rather more certain that the grain size is different. But I don't understand.'

'If the powders are different – ' I said, 'and only forensic examination could tell you for sure – then either the murderer didn't know what powder George Muir used or how much of it he had available— '

'And who would or wouldn't know such a thing?' the Sergeant asked.

'I hadn't finished. Or,' I said, 'the murderer knew that *Poudre T* is a rather slow-burning powder. He'd want something a bit livelier if he was going to build up pressure for a good bang before the lid blew off the pot. Possibly H Two-forty or Hercules Bullseye, intended for pistols.'

'And plenty of it?'

'That's for sure,' I said. 'If George Muir killed himself accidentally, or if somebody else used his powder to do the job, he or they probably finished emptying one tin and opened another.'

'So where would the other one be? The widow removed it in her orgy of tidying?'

'I doubt that,' I said. 'She wouldn't open tins. She'd have lifted what there was, very gingerly, and dropped it into this cardboard box. If George Muir killed himself accidentally, he probably threw away the empty tin himself. The dustbin's probably been emptied several times since then. If he was murdered, the killer carried the empty tin away with him.'

'Or with her,' said Sergeant Bedale. She leaned back against my work-bench and looked me in the eye. 'I'm not convinced by theories involving fuses and timers. I find it easier to visualise a thin electric wire leading through that hole. Can you point me towards anybody other than Mrs Muir who could have set up a trap and removed the evidence before we came?'

'Easily,' I said, without thinking.

'Go ahead.'

It was too late to retreat. I spoke up reluctantly. 'Alistair Young,' I said.

She nodded. Evidently she had read the earlier reports with care. 'First on the scene after the widow,' she said thoughtfully. 'Motive?'

I explained that George Muir's will had provided for an exchange of houses. 'Mr Young tried to foist his own pet surveyor onto Mrs Muir,' I said. 'If he'd got away with it he'd have been able to move his family into a bigger house – which they sorely need – at very little cost to himself. Indirectly, he expected to benefit to the tune of some thousands of pounds.'

'Anybody else?'

Some silly reticence, or a mistaken sense of male loyalty, restrained me from mentioning George Muir's amorous tendencies. I preferred to interpret the Sergeant's question as being directed towards opportunity rather than motive. 'Not to my knowledge. But the Muirs were very careless about keys. The front-door key was usually on the ledge over the door, ready for the handyman or the daily woman. That sort of arrangement usually becomes public knowledge. Anybody could have got in and out.'

The Sergeant came away from the bench, revealing a streak of grease across her grey flannel backside. 'So anybody could have got in to set up such an arrangement while the house was empty,' she said. 'Anybody could have lurked outside the window, to make an electrical connection at the moment George Muir arrived at the work-bench. But how could anybody other than Mr or Mrs Young count on getting in and out again to remove the evidence? The studio windows can't be opened more than a few inches.'

'The evidence would only be a wire,' I pointed out. 'It could be pulled out through the window within a few seconds. No need to go inside again. With so much paint and turpentine in the place, one of the windows would have stood open much of the time.'

'Perhaps.' She dropped the tin of powder back in to the carton and picked up the pot. 'I'll have to take this lot with me,' she said. 'I'll give you a receipt.'

'All right.'

I expected her to pick up the carton and make one of her ungracious exits, leaving me standing around like a prat. Instead, she stood looking at me uncertainly.

'Captain— '

'Mister,' I said.

'Mister Cunningham . . . ' She paused, in the grip of some internal struggle. 'What . . . in your personal opinion . . . what do you think I should do now?'

The question took me aback and I wondered whether she was testing me again. 'Don't ask me,' I said. 'Ask one of your colleagues. Or your husband.'

'My husband wouldn't be a whole lot of help.'

'Isn't he in the Force?'

'He is. But he'd rather see me out of it. He wants me to stay at home and be a good little housewife and slipper-warmer. You set this ball rolling and now I'm supposed to pick it up and carry it. What would you advise? What would you do in my place?'

Her troubled look and the surprising uncertainty in her usually positive eyes were appealing. I was a long way from succumbing to her new, plaintive femininity, but I found myself disliking her rather less. 'I know damn all about rules and procedures,' I said carefully, 'and even less about the personalities you have to cope with. I can only say that I think, on balance, that George Muir was probably murdered. If you decide that you agree, I don't see that your conscience would allow you to report otherwise. Or are you afraid of being unpopular?'

'I'm unpopular enough already,' she said wryly. I could believe it. Her usual self-confidence would make enemies, especially among male colleagues competing with her for promotion.

'Look at it this way,' I said. I stopped, uncertain of what I had been going to say. I went on, picking slowly through the maze. 'Assume that there was a murder. It wasn't one of those casual, roadside killings which must be the most difficult to solve. But it wasn't a habitual criminal's murder, so you can't expect any help from informers. Somebody wanted George Muir dead, that's a starting point. That same somebody must have taken some deliberate steps and he – or she, if you like – couldn't have done so without leaving some evidence somewhere. My advice would be to go on a bit further before making a report. You might find enough evidence to justify asking for forensic backup.

'It seems to me,' I finished, 'that your choice lies between that and taking the easy option . . . confirming George Muir's death as an accident.'

She nodded. 'That's just what I was thinking,' she said. She paused and then added, 'Thank you.'

'Don't mention it,' I said. For once, I meant the trite phrase. It seemed to me that I had said nothing beyond the most mundane and obvious.

Henry arrived alone at Three Oaks on the Friday morning. Isobel had suffered a flare-up of toothache during the night and had gone off to the Dental Hospital in Dundee. Henry brought apologetic messages.

I was watching Beth and Jason on the grass at the time. They worked well together. They were hardly up to competition standard yet, but they were developing a relationship. I had already tested them at an evening roost-shoot of wood-pigeon and they would make an adequate team for a day's picking-up and no doubt gain experience and cement their relationship in the process. Dogs are quick to sense a pecking order and Jason had already decided for himself that I was the pack leader with Beth as an acceptable deputy.

'Don't keep whistling at him unless he needs help,' I told Beth. 'Let him learn to use his nose.' And to Henry, 'Quite right. Isobel has to be on her best form tomorrow. But I'll have to give Gargany a last-minute polish for her. She's inclined to get above herself if she isn't reminded of her proper place at regular intervals.'

'Isobel?' Henry said. 'How true!'

'Gargany, you ass,' I retorted. 'I'll take her onto The Moss now.'

'Can we come?' Beth asked quickly.

After a second of consideration, I nodded. The runs were clean, the puppies fed and the dogs in various stages of training had been put through their exercises. 'Hattie can mind the baby,' I said. 'Come and shoot for us, Henry?'

'With the Dickson?' Henry said.

'If you insist.'

Gargany was one of those lucky chances which can happen to all of us but which usually only happen to others. She was a black and white springer bitch, the product of a litter sired by Samson out of one of my best brood bitches. There is a limit to how many young dogs a trainer can manage and I had intended to keep only one bitch pup out of the litter to train and sell as a working dog. Gargany had not been my choice. But while the rest of the pups had sold and sold well, Gargany, because of asymmetrical markings which gave her a peculiarly lopsided appearance, had failed to fetch her price. I had started bringing her on to sell as a worker. After a slow start she had suddenly shown talent and even the promise of future stardom. Tomorrow should see her take her first step towards champion status.

We crossed the road and walked towards The Moss over a stubble field, still unploughed thanks to a wet autumn. An early frost had thawed, but the light was still bright and clear. There was the chance of a covey of partridges and we had permission to shoot game as well as vermin, so I sent Gargany out. She soon settled into an efficient quartering pattern, Jason, as befitted his function in life, remained at Beth's heel, watching Gargany's work with an air of superiority. In his view, spaniels had been provided by nature to be his labourers.

Henry loaded the gun and walked between us. I felt a pang of jealousy. I was still in the honeymoon stage with that gun. I think that I would rather have seen Beth hanging on Henry's arm than the Dickson.

There was time to chat. 'I had a George Muir painting once,' Henry said.

Gargany was getting too far out on my left. I gave her the turn whistle. 'What happened to it?' I asked.

'Sold it when Isobel wanted capital to go into business with you. My investments were low at the time, but the painting fetched about a hundred times what I paid for it.'

'Golly!' Beth said.

A hare got up in front of us. True to their training, both dogs froze. Henry mounted the gun and then, to my relief, held his fire. I prefer hares alive rather than jugged.

'Tomorrow,' I said to Beth, 'about the most unsettling thing that could happen to you would be for Jason to bring you a wounded hare. If you lose your nerve and start wringing your hands, you'll just be making bad worse. Pick it up by the hind legs and give it a good whack on the back of the head – remind me, I'll give you a "priest" to take with you. And tell the silly beggar who shot it to leave hares alone until he's learned to shoot straight.'

'On Lord Craill's shoot, he'll be a duke or an earl or something,' Beth objected.

'Possibly. Or the local dustman. Craill isn't fussy – lords don't need to be snobs. Tick the culprit off anyway.'

We had reached the hedge which bounded The Moss. It was threaded with a fence of rusty barbed wire. I held the wire down for Beth to step over. 'Too bad about your painting,' I told Henry.

He shrugged while unloading the gun and dropped a cartridge. 'Isobel never liked it much anyway. It showed a terrier killing rats. Full of action but a little on the gruesome side.' He grunted as he picked up the dropped cartridge and again as he stepped over the wire. 'It was funny how I came by it. Years and years ago, I was at an auction. I only went because there was a table for sale that I rather fancied. It went for more than I could manage so that I was left sitting on some spare cash. There were two of George Muir's paintings in the sale and I rather fancied one of them. This was before he was known.

'When the other painting came up, it was bought by a big, fat chap. I noticed that the only person bidding against him was a small woman, and I'd seen the two of them together before the auction started. It puzzled me at first, because if they'd co-operated they could have got it much more cheaply. Then I realised that they must be working for the painter. It's an old racket. What,' he asked me abruptly, 'is the value of something?'

I had been on the point of moving on, but Henry had suddenly caught my interest. A phrase which I had heard came into my mind. 'What the next fools' going to pay for it?' I suggested.

'Wrong. It's what the last ten fools paid for something similar. If you're Joe Snooks, the good but unknown artist, or if you have a corner in his work, you put examples of it up for auction and have them bought back at steadily increasing prices. Eventually, the record of prices fetched establishes that the true value of a Joe Snooks painting is umpty pounds. Then you start letting them go. It costs you the auctioneer's commission each time, but that's money well spent if your work fetches its full value while you're still around to enjoy it instead of after you're dead.

'I was standing behind the two. I joined in the bidding when the picture I wanted came up. Each of them probably thought that the successful bid was the other's and they looked baffled when it was knocked down to me. What I paid for it was probably over the odds at the time, but I liked it and I reckoned that if they went on conspiring to inflate the values I'd get my money back in the end. And so I did,' Henry finished with satisfaction.

'The fat chap,' I said. 'Did he have a built-in frown and jowls?'

'As far as I remember. You know him?'

'Alistair Young,' I said. 'He has a tiny wife. And Hattie told me that he'd been a friend of George Muir for yonks. Now we know why.'

We set off across The Moss. The rough ground was a magnet in winter for both game and vermin. After fifty yards, Gargany put two rabbits out of a gorse bush. Henry missed the first but killed the second dead.

'Missed in front,' he said. 'For all its weight, this thing swings faster than you expect. Well balanced, I suppose.'

The dogs were sitting tight. 'Do you want Gargany to pick it?' Beth asked.

'I want her to be reminded that not every shot means a retrieve for her,' I said. 'Send Jason.'

She sent the Labrador. Gargany looked at me with reproach. Jason brought the limp rabbit. Beth handed it to me to bag and we set off again.

Twenty minutes later we had worked our way round to near the patch of open woodland which formed the heart of The Moss. Fringed with reedy, wet ground and comprising scattered clumps of alders undergrown with brambles and heather and sudden patches of gorse, I had found it a valuable training area even when poached to emptiness by some of my less reputable neighbours.

A cock pheasant exploded from under Beth's feet, making her squeak with surprise. Henry was almost caught flatfooted, but he recovered, swung and fired. The pheasant turned over and dropped among the reeds.

Both the dogs and Beth were looking at me in restrained eagerness. I nodded to Beth. She gave Jason the signal with professional clarity and he cantered forward. But he sniffed at the reeds for a moment and then moved uncertainly towards the jungle. Beth whistled. He checked but went on again.

'Leave him,' I said. 'I think we've got a runner.'

'It didn't look like a runner.'

'When you can't see, trust the dog,' I told her. 'If you're lucky, he's following the scent.' Privately

I rather hoped that Gargany would wipe Jason's eye. It might teach them both a lesson.

'I don't suppose that Jason's ever picked a pheasant before,' Beth said.

She was probably right. Jason seemed puzzled. He was young and Edgar Lawrence's ground was hardly in pheasant country. 'All right,' I said. 'Call him in.'

Beth whistled and Jason came reluctantly back to her. I sent Gargany. The spaniel picked up a scent and vanished.

We waited. There was little warmth in the low sunshine but no bite in the breeze.

'I like this gun,' Henry said suddenly. 'How would you like to swap it for Isobel's share of your year's profit?'

'Isobel might have something to say about that,' I pointed out.

'I could coax her.'

'John's going to keep his gun,' Beth said firmly. 'I want him to have it. And you are a nasty old man, Henry, calling my uncle a fraud and then trying to diddle John.'

'I wasn't,' Henry protested. 'I made him a good offer. And I didn't say anything about fraud. As far as I know, there's nothing illegal in getting a friend to buy your own pictures for you. Nobody was forced to pay the new prices and if they did they still made a good investment.'

'Alistair Young really is a fraud, though,' I said. 'I couldn't avoid telling Sergeant Bedale about his try-on over Hattie's house and I could see her mind starting to work, just as clearly as if her thoughts were in a cartoonist's bubble above her head. "Next-door neighbour. Bound to know about the key above the door. First on the scene after the widow, who would have been too shaken to notice something like a wire leading out of the window." That sort of thing.'

'From what Isobel relayed to me,' Henry said, 'he has an alibi of a sort for the time of the explosion.'

'His wife and his brother-in-law,' Beth said. 'He could get them to say anything.'

Gargany came out of the jungle with a limp cock pheasant in her jaws, looking very pleased with herself. She presented it, sitting, to Beth. I took it and felt it carefully, but the rib-cage was intact. The bird had not been bitten, it had been mortally shot, but had still had a few yards left in it.

'Would Alistair Young kill, just to give himself an opportunity to try to swindle the widow?' I asked.

'We don't know what other motive he might have had,' Beth said. She looked at me meaningfully.

Somehow I could not see the petite and skinny Mrs Young as meat for the predatory George Muir. 'More to the point,' I said, 'he had the best opportunity to remove anything incriminating before the police arrived.'

'He didn't act very guilty,' Beth said.

'That sort of aggressiveness often covers up a bad conscience. Let's move on. You'd better try Jason on that pheasant in the open.'

Beth looked at me in uncertainty. 'I thought that you taught dogs to ignore quarry which had already been handled,' she said. 'This will have my scent all over it.'

'That's for workers,' I said. 'You're planning to compete with Jason; and they sometimes plant handled game as a final test in a run-off.'

I hid the dead bird between two clumps of heather some fifty yards away and Beth handled Jason onto it. The young Labrador hesitated and then lifted the bird. His tail was thrashing as he came back. 'From now on, that's a scent he'll never forget,' I said.

'Why would Lawrence be training the dog competition-style if it was promised to a wildfowler?' Henry asked.

I shrugged. I did not want to voice the most obvious reason, but it was difficult to think of any others.

Seven

Breeding and training gundogs may be one of the least tedious means of earning a living for anyone of my inclinations; but it is a way of life which cannot be suspended at short notice. Dogs have to be guarded against theft or malicious attack, fed, exercised, humanised and entertained. In addition, phones have to be answered and visitors confronted. With Hattie and Isobel going off to the field trial and Beth coming with me to Lord Craill's shoot, Henry stepped into the breach as often before. He always grumbled, but I believe that he enjoyed those occasional days of peaceful responsibility. Whenever we returned, we found all in perfect order and Henry almost sober.

Beth and I made a point of being at the beaters' assembly area before the appointed time. Lord Craill was served by a keeper who had at one time been a warrant officer in the Scots Guards, and he ran each shoot with the discipline and precision of a military exercise. Any team prefers to know exactly what it should do and when, so the estate was never short of beaters. If the Guns were still milling about and chatting when the birds began to come over, that was their loss; it seldom happened again after the first drive.

Lord Craill, who was a pleasant young man with sandy hair and a slight stammer, owned a considerable acreage of land in Fife. This was mostly too scattered to be of use for pheasants, but he had contrived to bring together the sporting rights to four arable farms on well-wooded and contoured ground.

On such hilly land, Beth was usually out of my sight; and with only two pickers-up serving a line of eight guns, I was too busy during the drives to keep an eye on her. Some of the guests were second-rate shots and I had to watch each bird to judge whether it was pricked and a potential runner. When I caught her between drives she looked anxious but claimed to be more concerned as to whether I was getting chilled in the frosty air; and I was relieved to hear one guest remark to Lord Craill that it restored his faith in the coming generation to see good Labrador-handling by a pretty teenager. After that, I could relax and concentrate on working Samson and Brockleton. The spaniels were fractious – they would have preferred to be with the beating line. The 'teenager' comment I filed away, to tease Beth.

It would have been usual for the pickers-up to lunch on beer and sandwiches with the beaters but Lord Craill, as he often did, invited me to join his guests. Beth, who would probably have preferred the humbler lunch, was added to the invitation.

Rather than waste valuable shooting time by a return to the Big House, a buffet meal had been laid out on a trestle table in a large barn. Wallace, the head keeper, had bolted his own meal and had appointed himself to preside over the drinks table. This, and a basilisk glare at anyone taking more than a single sip from a flask, enabled him to ensure that the Guns would face the afternoon in a state of reasonable sobriety. What to the guests was primarily a social event was, in the keeper's view, an occasion for filling the game cart and thereby paying for next year's birds. When I collected a single beer from him and a soda for Beth, he unbent enough to praise her work with Jason.

I joined Beth where she was sitting shyly on one of the straw bales which had been ranged round the walls of the barn. Several of the guests paused to talk with us about dogs but most moved on. An American, who seemed to know very few of the other guests, settled beside us. He introduced himself as Kenneth James Boyce from Houston. 'Most folks,' he said, 'call me Kenny.' He was a small man and slim, remarkably so for a Texan, with high cheekbones and a pointed chin. We compared spaniels with the Shorthaired Pointers which were his usual shooting companions.

'I'm only here by chance,' he said when we seemed to have exhausted the subject. 'I was supposed to be here and gone by now, but my passport came up missing some time back, stolen I guess, and you wouldn't believe the time it takes to get a replacement.'

'It takes even longer over here,' I said.

'Is that so?' he said. 'If you say so. Seems hard to believe, though. Anyways, I came over to visit our subsidiary here in Fife and I was having a dinner with our sales manager over this side at Braidie Castle Hotel – I'm staying there. We met up with Lord Craill and fell to talking over a drink. It seems that Bruce was already coming to this shoot. When Lord Craill heard that I was a hunter he invited me to come along as an extra.

'Well, I sure did want to try your driven pheasants, but I've read about it and I had an idea how an extra guest could louse it up for all the others. But Bruce said that he had a whole lot of work stacked up and he'd be happy to give up his place to me. Lord Craill said that that was great and Bruce could come here next time. Bruce let me borrow his gun.'

'Are you enjoying it as much as you thought you would?' Beth asked.

'It's great,' he said. 'But I'm not doing so good with a strange gun. It's side by side, you see, and I'm used to an over and under. Yet the chokes aren't any different to speak of. I don't differ much from Bruce in build and my eye seems to come in lie with the rib.'

This was a problem I had come across before. 'You're missing under?' I asked him.

'Seems like it. Bruce fixed me up with some of his reloads, but they feel pretty much like my own.'

'You may be aiming low with your left hand because you're used to the deeper fore-end on an over-under. Try stuffing a handkerchief into the palm of your left glove.'

'That could be right,' he said thoughtfully. 'Darn it, I should of thought of that.'

The repeated mentions of 'Bruce' combined with the other circumstances suddenly threw up an identity in my mind. 'Would that be Bruce Fullerton?' I asked. 'He works for an American concern and I met him on this shoot last year.'

'That's the man,' he said. 'You know him?'

'I've met him a couple of times. I helped him to get his dog back.'

'That was you, was it? He was mighty glad to recover that dog. A handsome critter though not what I'd want for a shooting dog. Seemed to me that Bruce was as much cut up about the dog as about his wife. He was over in the States at the time, learning about our new line of products. The old days when a salesman could be selling perfume one month and computers the next are long gone. In the hi-tech field, a sales manager has to be ready to snap back with the answer to any question the customer can throw at him.'

'This was in Texas?' I asked idly.

Ken Boyce shook his head and made a face of disgust. 'New York. The Big Apple. The Rotten Apple, I call it, but you have to go where the work is.' He shook his head again, this time sadly. 'Bruce has had it tough. She was his second wife and he thought the world of her. First part of his stay he was on the phone home most nights, from his hotel room or mine, trying to make up after some spat they'd had. I guess the fault couldn't have been all on her side, because he was no monk. Rented a car one weekend and said that he was driving up for a skiing weekend in Vermont but I don't know how much skiiing he did. She-ing more like. Begging your pardon, young lady,' he added to Beth.

'Just after that, I heard him yelling at his wife again on the phone and he told me she'd threatened to have his dog put down. That would sure as hell be one lousy trick. But I guess she didn't do it if you found the dog for him. Maybe she still has a soft centre after all. And, next thing, he got word that she'd been killed in a fall. He flew back as soon as he could get away and I followed on when my new passport came through.'

Beth was set to probe further into the tragedy of Bruce Fullerton's marriage, but the intractable Mr Wallace was making it clear that lunch was over and that the Guns had better make their way to the next stand or the birds would be driven over vacant pegs.

I had time for a word with the small Texan before

the last drive of the day. He gave me his card and showed me his bulging left palm. 'It took two handkerchiefs and my tie,' he said. 'Feels kind of clumsy, but it did the trick. I'm swatting them good.' He gave me his card. 'Any time you're over in the States look me up. We'll shoot some skeet together and I'll show you how pointers work on quail.'

My Sunday class for aspiring trainers and their dogs would not come round again until the following week. On all other Sabbaths it was our habit to give ourselves an easy day. A respite from the rigors of training did us all good, the dogs no less than the people.

Puppies still had to be fed, runs cleaned and the dogs given some free-running exercise, but when those duties were done we lit the sitting room fire and the three partners and Henry settled down for a drink and a *post mortem* on the previous day's events. We tried to include Hattie in the fellowship of the group, but our conversation was necessarily centred around dogs and shooting and field trials, all of which were areas so foreign to her that they might have been in outer space. So, feeling rather left out of things but taking it in good part, she had finished the housework, left our lunch in a slow oven and taken Mona for a walk, well wrapped against the chill of another frosty day.

'Despite whatever you lot may think,' Isobel said, 'I am not a bad loser. But I resent being pushed back into second place by a dog which has had surgery on its vocal chords.'

'If you're sure,' I said, 'you could have lodged an objection. That's a disqualification offence under the new rules.'

'How could I be sure?' Isobel asked grumpily. 'I wasn't there at the time of the operation. All I know is that the blighter was usually put out last season because he couldn't keep quiet, and yesterday he hardly even yelped when he was trodden on. But I didn't want to start a feud, let alone put down a twenty-five quid deposit when the owner could probably produce a certificate to say that the operation had been for nodules.'

Isobel was drinking shandy, a sure sign that her modest success had been celebrated the previous evening although Hattie had been reticent on the subject. Beth was on Babycham and Henry and I were drinking canned beer.

'Not to worry,' I said. 'Second place will qualify her for an Open Stake as soon as we think she's ready for it. Brockleton worked well, by the way. His owner can pick him up tomorrow. I've phoned him.'

'Thank God for small mercies,' Isobel said. 'How did Jason get on?'

'He was beautiful,' Beth said. (Henry and Isobel looked at each other and raised their eyebrows.) 'No, truly,' she said. 'He was a bit sticky at first. He seemed to think that he was still in training and that somebody was waiting to skelp him for the least error. Once he realised that he was there to do a job, he went like a dream.'

'Allowing for an understandable exaggeration,' I said, 'that's quite true. I had a grandstand view across the valley on the last drive and for most of it the birds weren't coming over my end of the line so I was free to watch you. I saw you handle him out onto the scent of a strong runner and then leave him to work it out for himself. You were good and he was even better.'

Beth blushed like the schoolgirl she so much resembled. 'Honestly?' she said.

'Honestly. Keep working with him and we'll enter you for a Puppy Stake after Christmas.'

Beth's blush turned to scarlet.

Isobel chose to be amused. 'You'll take it in your stride,' she said. She got up and replaced her empty glass with a strong gin and tonic.

'Better now?' I asked her.

'I can feel the faint possibility of survival creeping up on me. Let Jason make a name for himself,' she said to Beth, 'and we'll maybe get some useful stud fees for him.'

I yawned. It was very quiet in the room. 'Let's stick to one breed,' I said. 'We don't go in for Labradors.'

'And I don't want Jason learning any nasty habits,' Beth said. Her face was straight but there was a mischievous gleam in her eye.

Henry's long shape was stretched out in an easy chair so that his legs nearly bisected the room. 'I don't know why you should consider such habits nasty,' he said. 'The human race seems to be thriving on them. And according to the Indian scriptures – Indian Indian, I mean, not American Indian – women get eight times more pleasure out of sex than men do.'

'That could be true,' Isobel said.

'Perhaps that's why you used to go around with a smile on your face,' Henry suggested.

'And perhaps that's why I'm frowning now,' Isobel replied.

Beth snorted with laughter and got Babycham down her nose. I mopped her with my handkerchief and then lent it to her.

'I don't know why that should remind me,' Isobel

said, ' – or perhaps I do – but I saw your Bruce Fullerton at the trial yesterday, John. There was a face among the spectators which rang a faint bell and later it came back to me that it had belonged to a client, years ago when I was working as a vet. He had a cocker spaniel, in those days, which was always ripping itself on barbed wire and having to be stitched up. Then the name Fullerton popped into my head and I realised that it must be the same man.'

'Small, skinny and with a face sharp enough to skin a rabbit?' I said.

'That sounds like him. I didn't have time to look and, to tell the truth, I remember his dog better than I remember him. He saw me looking at him and glared at me so I had to look away and the judges called us into the line again just then. But I glimpsed him later on, fawning around that stout, blonde woman who always enters the huge springer with the mainly white coat.'

'Men!' Beth said. 'We met his boss at Lord Craill's shoot yesterday and he said that Mr Fullerton was working.'

'He was working all right,' Isobel said. 'And I know what he was working for.'

'Knowing the lady, he probably got it,' said Henry. 'Can't think why he's bothering. Only been a widower for a month or two.'

'Not used to the celibate life,' I suggested. 'The fact that he's already been married twice suggests that he doesn't like to go without his little comforts.'

We relaxed in our various seats and silence fell, broken only when one or the other of us gave a small sound of amusement. The stout, blonde handler was not respected in the trials community and the picture of the undersized Bruce Fullerton in her amorous clutches, which should have evoked disapproval, was only food for ribaldry and mirth. It was one of those peaceful moments which should always precede Sunday lunch. It also happened to be the last peaceful moment of the day and for several days afterwards.

I was looking once again at the wall above the fireplace and trying to visualise our painting in position when Hattie appeared in the door, bringing with her the chill of the great outdoors. She was showing agitation and we all looked at her. Mona hobbled between us to the warmth of the fire and pushed her grizzled jowls almost into the chimney.

'Somebody,' Hattie said, 'is prowling around near the dogs. He ducked down behind one of the kennels as I came in at the gates. And such a bedlam of barking I'm wondering you didn't hear it. I had a job pretending not to notice, but I thought that you might not want me to scare him off.'

In the few years since we formed our partnership we had had two thefts, a poisoning and an attempt to steal a service off Samson; and at the last annual stocktaking our accountant had drawn our attention to the fact that our valuable and perishable livestock represented a much larger portion of our assets than did such items as kennels and equipment. So we were acutely aware of the vulnerability of the kennels. We reacted as might a colony of rabbits on the intrusion of a ferret.

As I bolted into the hall, Beth was actually treading on my heels. I wanted her out of harm's way. 'Take our car,' I told her. 'Drive down to the road.

If anyone's left another car handy, you may be able to block it in. But don't take any chances.'

'And the same to you,' she said.

I pushed the car keys at her. 'If you're in any doubt stay clear, but try to see where he goes.'

As Hattie had said, the dogs were barking their heads off. Normally they would have fallen quiet at my approach, but not when I came tearing across the grass and round the groups of kennels at full gallop. As best I could see in that almost photographic glimpse, nothing was out of place. The gates to the runs seemed to be closed. None of the dogs was eating strange meat or acting as though a stranger was hiding inside its kennel. The excitement had brought them all into the runs, but there was one notable absentee. I checked my pace slightly and hurried over the grass.

Across the drive from the hedge, an old wall formed the boundary to the road. Between the mown grass and the wall was an area which had held some old lilac trees and a flowering cherry. Beth had underplanted it with shrubs and had then left it to turn wild with whatever undergrowth cared to seed itself. It formed a haven for small birds, a floriferous barrier between ourselves and the road and a useful patch for giving puppies their first taste of searching in cover. It was also the one place where an intruder would hide – with the added advantage, from our viewpoint, that the wall was topped with barbed wire. Once in, he was trapped.

As I neared the first shrubs, Jason bolted out with his tail between his legs. I skidded to a halt. The young Labrador nearly bowled me over and then twined himself around my legs, seeking reassurance. He was panting feverishly and salivating. I was out of breath myself. I patted him and rubbed his neck until he was calmer and then walked to the edge of the cover. He followed me at heel, but very reluctantly.

'Where is he?' I asked softly.

Jason balked at re-entering the cover but he moved to a gap between two young rhododendrons, growled once and pointed like a bird-dog. It was enough. I waved him towards the house and he shot away.

'Are you coming out or do I have to come in and get you?' I asked.

There was no answer.

I worked my way round the rhododendrons, treading down dead nettles and long grass, and pushed aside an overgrown broom, spattering myself with drops of melted frost. The soles of a pair of muddy brown-leather boots were facing me. I kicked one of them hard on the ankle. 'Come out, come out, whoever you are,' I said, still puffing.

A man's figure, in blue jeans and a heavy sweater, began to back out from under a large ceanothus. He began slowly to straighten, then suddenly snapped upright and swung a fist at my face. It was more a panicky gesture than a serious attempt at assault.

I was still not wholly fit and it had been several years since I had used my skills, but you never forget unarmed combat training when it has been drummed into you by a sergeant-major seconded from the SAS and impatient to get back to his unit. I was still wondering what to do when I found that I had ducked aside – too slowly, his fist had flicked the end of my nose – and chopped backhand at where I knew that it would hurt the most.

He doubled over and held himself. I could have killed or crippled him with ease, but there was no need. He was ideally positioned for an incapacitating hold. Within two seconds I was holding one of his wrists between his legs while my other hand had a grip on the scruff of his neck. He tried to struggle but I bumped his head a few times against the trunk of one of the lilacs and jerked his wrist up against the tender area until he saw wisdom. Then I marched him, doubled up and helpless, out of the bushes and towards the house. He said nothing except to utter a low, moaning sound.

Henry and Isobel were still at the front door. Beth, who had recognised the car which was waiting in the road, had returned and was just bringing our car to rest behind a third car from which Sergeant Bedale was already emerging, crisp as ever but looking somehow more hesitant than usual.

'What goes on?' the Sergeant asked interestedly. She seemed to be in no hurry to interfere.

'Just caught an intruder,' I said. I had got my breath back. 'He was trying to steal one of our dogs.' It always helps to get your own story in first.

Beth had erupted out of our car, leaving the door open and the engine running. She stooped to look at my captive's face. 'But that's my cousin Edgar,' she said.

'I know,' I told her. 'I've seen him at the trials.'

I released my hold. He let go of himself cautiously and once he was quite sure that nothing was going to fall off he straightened up. Like his cousin, he was slim and dark, but he had close-set eyes – the mark of the natural predator – and teeth like those of a rodent.

'I wasn't stealing anything,' he said sullenly. 'You came to my place and you took away the wrong dog.'

Beth made a faint sound of distress.

'We took the right dog,' I said. 'If you don't agree, you have your remedy in the courts.'

'Why should I put myself at the mercy of the legal sharks? You took the wrong dog. I came to swap them over. Then it would have been up to you to spend the time and money raising an action.' He adopted a whining tone. 'I wasn't doing anything wrong, I was only rectifying a mistake. You had no right to attack me. I can have you up for that.'

'I understand what you're saying,' I said. 'I don't agree with a word of it, but I can see what you mean. What I don't understand is why you should care enough about one damn dog to kill your uncle for possession of him.'

My words, which seemed to emerge from me of their own volition and without conscious intent on my part, stunned all those present, including myself, into silence. Even the air was still. Edgar Lawrence drooped back against the wall of the house with his mouth open. Beth was looking at me oddly but also with concern.

'You're bleeding,' she said.

I touched my nose and found it tender. My finger came away bloody. 'He took a poke at me,' I said.

Henry and Isobel, who had been looking from one to the other of us like spectators at a tennis match, waited expectantly for the next development. Sergeant Bedale was also looking at me, but with what seemed to be dawning hope. 'I could hold him for that,' she said, 'while we look into the other matter.'

Edgar Lawrence was the first to recover his voice. 'I didn't do any such thing,' he said hoarsely.

'Which thing?' I asked him.

'Neither of them, you bastard.' He switched his eyes back to the Sergeant. 'Are you a police officer?'

'I am.'

'Then I'm charging this man with assault.'

'It seems to me that you have some explaining to do yourself,' the Sergeant said.

Edgar came away from the wall and glared at me. 'All right, so I wanted my dog back. I've got my ambitions, same as the next man. I've made up a champion once. It felt great at the time but, later, I didn't feel that I'd gained anything. Rather, I'd lost something. We all need something to look forward to, to work towards, to dream about. You understand?'

There was a faint murmur of assent. We were not sympathetic but we all knew about dreams.

'Well, I'd dreamed mine and it was gone. To make up another dog would have been less of a thrill. That left me with only one ambition, one dream. I wanted a dual champion. Show and Field Trials. For the first time, I had my hands on a young dog which might have done it. Jason. He has talent and he's going to be a looker.

'I ran my best bitch in an Open Stake yesterday. She's good, but she'll never win a prize in a show. And when I was pushed out of the money, I knew that Jason could have pulled it off. Not yet, but in a year or two.

'But I'd no need to kill to get him. Now that I know the sort of pups Farthingale Bonus can throw when he's put to my bitch, I can scrape up the money for another service and start over again. And I can do it.' He looked round our faces. 'My God! You don't believe me!'

I said 'No.' I meant that I didn't believe that he could do it. He was suffering from *folie de grandeur.* The odds were stacked against him. The same sire and dam might never produce a similar pup again and, if they did, he was not the man to partner it to victory. His own failings would defeat them. But he would be happy, living in hope.

Edgar had had enough of arguing his case to hostile faces. He put his head down and darted suddenly towards the front gates.

Sergeant Bedale lifted her skirt and took off after him. In flat-heeled shoes she had a rare turn of speed for a woman, and Edgar may have been slowed down by some discomfort in his parts. She caught him halfway across the grass and attempted a very masculine Rugby tackle, but he handed her off and fled on through the gates.

The Sergeant rolled over and sat up as I got to her. Beyond the gates we heard a car start. I helped the Sergeant to her feet. She was unhurt, but she had been unlucky in her fall and the neat grey suit, which had been painstakingly cleaned of the oily smudge, was now plastered with fresh dog-dirt. She hardly noticed. We walked back together to where the others were still clustered in a stunned group around the door.

'Where's your phone?' the Sergeant asked urgently. 'I must get on to the local force. If Edgar Lawrence murdered his uncle— '

'But he didn't,' Beth said quietly.

Hattie had appeared in the front doorway. 'What are you saying?' she demanded. 'Of course he did no such thing.'

I sighed. 'I'm sorry, Hattie,' I said. 'I didn't want you to hear it like this. We just didn't want you subjected to any more harassment until we could be sure, one way or the other. But I was never satisfied that your husband's death was accidental.'

Hattie just nodded. 'No more was I,' she said.

The Sergeant, now looking more complete with

her eternal notebook in her hand, stared at Hattie. 'You never said anything to the officers,' she said.

'I told them that George was far too careful to blow himself up like that. If they cared to ignore me, I'd nothing more to tell them. I could have been wrong. And if I'd set them thinking, they'd as likely have started to picture me creeping up behind him and tossing a lighted match over his shoulder or some such foolishness. So I told them what I was sure of and no more than that. My thoughts were my own until now. But if anyone harmed George, it surely wasn't Edgar. George was speaking to him on the phone only minutes before it happened.'

'Which one of them made the call?' Sergeant Bedale asked quickly. She was still eager to get at the phone but hesitated to spread the alarm in the face of Hattie's certainty.

'George did. So Edgar was at home and he'd have needed to be in that Concorde to cover the distance in the time.'

'But that doesn't matter,' Beth said unhappily. 'He wouldn't have had to be there.'

'Well, then, there's another reason,' Hattie said. 'George was thinking of changing his will. His paintings had been making good prices and he felt that he'd not be robbing me if he left Edgar a legacy of some money. I was agreeable. But George never got around to it. Every time he was on the point of doing it, the silly boy put his back up over something trivial and George would delay again.

'Mind you,' Hattie said warming to her theme, 'I'm not saying that Edgar wouldn't have been capable of killing his uncle. It's my opinion that the boy's a skellum through and through. But he's too much notion of the value of money to have done it before the will was changed.'

'Did he know that it hadn't been changed?' I asked.

'He knew fine,' Hattie said. 'George had made a point of it.'

'That seems to settle it for the moment,' the Sergeant said unhappily. She looked around the faces until she found mine. 'I need to have a word with you. In private. Can we use your sitting room again?'

I looked at the state of the Sergeant's clothing. 'I think we'd better use the kitchen,' I suggested.

The Sergeant fetched a flat package from her car and followed me into the kitchen, where two pans were simmering gently on the stove and a smell of roasting hung in the air. She wiped her feet carefully before entering the house, although she might have removed more of the mess if she had rolled on the mat. When she made for one of the soft, fireside chairs, I headed her towards one of the Windsor chairs by the table. At least it could be carried outside and hosed down. She blinked at me, her mind elsewhere, and put down the package.

'Hadn't you better clean yourself up a bit before you sit down?' I asked her. In the warm atmosphere of the kitchen the Sergeant, to put it bluntly, was beginning to offend.

She glanced down and slapped absently at a stem of grass which clung to her skirt. She examined her fingers and seemed to realise her state for the first time. She uttered a mildly rude but apt word in the tone of voice which suggests that the speaker's patience is being tested beyond endurance, moved to the sink and washed her hands. I gave her a roll of paper towels, but what she needed was a bath, a laundry and a visit to the dry cleaner's.

While she dabbed ineffectually at her person she spoke, still in the same strained tone. 'I'm in a mess. You helped me to get into it and I hope you can help me to get out again.'

'I will if I can,' I said. 'For starters, would you like me to clean your back?'

She still had enough of her old spirit to look at me as though I were trying to get my hands on her for a cheap thrill. 'I can manage,' she said. 'I didn't mean that sort of mess.'

She hung her jacket over a chairback and swivelled her skirt round on her hips. While she dabbed and wiped, she spoke over her shoulder to me. There was now no trace of the over-confident officer who had so much irritated me. Instead there was a woman, worried and uncertain, seeking help and even perhaps a little comfort. I thought that I could detect in her unconscious body language more than a trace of the small girl who had once expected the big, strong man to solve every problem for her.

'You had me convinced that George Muir was murdered and that Alistair Young killed him,' she said.

'I agree with the first. I don't think that I ever told you the second,' I said.

'Maybe not. But what you implied convinced me. Perhaps you . . . we . . . were jumping to conclusions, or perhaps not. I still think that he may . . . ' She broke off and took several deep breaths before stumbling on. 'I don't know what to think. But, anyway, I decided that although any evidence he'd left in the Muir's house may have been scattered or destroyed, there might be some in his own. Wires, a detonating device, fuses, radio, anything like that. At least the tools and materials he'd used. If nothing else, I thought that he might still have a tin containing some pistol powder. He wouldn't put such a thing out with his rubbish. A hell of a bang in the municipal incinerator would attract just the sort of notice he wanted to avoid.

'None of my direct superiors was around on Friday so I took the chance to use what you might call the back door. The duty inspector knew no more than that I'd been told to look into George Muir's death, so I span him a tale – I must have been out of my mind – and he went after a search warrant. And he got it.'

'Ouch!' I said.

'Yes. God, how I wish they'd turned him down! Yesterday, I borrowed two men and a WDC and went out to serve the warrant. I thought, as you said yourself, that there had to be something.'

'And you found nothing?'

'I'm not sure whether we found anything or not,' she said. There was a quaver in her voice. 'We found nothing whatever directly related to the murder. But we did find something suspicious, tucked behind a chest of drawers. Mr Young was furious. I don't think that I ever saw anybody in such temper. He swore that he'd had them for years. He even suggested that they were his own work, but when I said that no doubt his wife could confirm it he backed off a bit. But he insisted that he was going to make an official complaint and also sue me personally. He claims that he knows everybody in the hierarchy between my inspector and God. Even if he doesn't . . . '

'In other words,' I said, 'he's going to kick up hell.'

'Exactly. And if he does . . . well, I've stepped out of line. I was told to make tactful enquiries and to report back. But I tried to be too clever. I thought that I could bring the case back to my superiors all neatly tied up with ribbon.' It was sackcloth and ashes time. If her hands had not been full of messy paper towels, she would have been wringing them. 'Now I've got egg all over my face unless I can stall him until he cools down enough to see that he'd be offering himself up to be pilloried by the media. Or . . . ' She stopped dead.

'Or what?' I said helpfully.

She suddenly made up her mind and began again in a rush. 'Or unless what I found had been stolen from George Muir's house. That could start a whole new ball game. If nothing else, it would be evidence that he'd made illicit entry into the Muir house. That might not mean that he'd set a trap for George Muir – he can only have wanted them for his own gratification – but it would justify the search.' She paused again and then lowered her voice. 'I want you to look in that package on the table. Tell me what you think. And I'm not even going to look round while you have them out.'

This was very intriguing. Without quite believing it, I could make a guess as to what was coming. Two flat sheets of cardboard had been tied together with tape. I untied the tape and opened the package.

It held more than a dozen sheets of heavy paper bearing watercolours or ink and wash drawings, all meticulously finished and detailed. The ladies depicted would have been easy to recognise; indeed I thought that I recognised two of them although I had only seen them in passing. Every detail was erotic to the point of being—

But no. I was on the point of writing that the pictures were pornographic, but somehow that would not have been true. They had been executed with charm and humour and even a sort of love. In their way, they were beautiful. If asked, I would have had to say that they were Art.

'I think I need to ask my fiancée about these,' I said.

The Sergeant almost turned round but thought better of it. 'Your fiancée? I'd forgotten that you were engaged to Miss Cattrell. I keep thinking of her as your daughter. Surely you won't show her . . . those!'

'She's mature enough to take it. She's twenty-six,' I said. 'No, on second thoughts, twenty-eight.'

'You had to think about it?' For a moment the old, superior amusement showed in her voice.

'Time goes so quickly when you're enjoying somebody,' I said.

'I thought that you were cradle-snatching.'

'People do. But remember that she was George Muir's niece.'

'That will make it worse for her.' The Sergeant sighed in the general direction of the window. 'Well, I suppose that they stop just short of the boundary of hard-core porn – which makes it more difficult to justify my removal of them – so you may as well go ahead. Don't blame me if she goes into shock. I was thinking that you might make a tactful approach to Mrs Muir.'

The idea of showing the sketches to Hattie made me shudder. I opened the kitchen door and called to Beth. She came out of the sitting room, turned for a last word with Hattie and then joined me.

'Isobel's gone out to finish that hedge,' she said. 'It's her form of doodling. I wish she'd leave it alone. I do it straighter than she does.'

'You can straighten it up tomorrow,' I told her. 'It'll recover in a year or two. Now, brace yourself and take a look at these. They were recovered from the Youngs' house.'

Beth looked down at the pictures which I had spread on the kitchen table. 'At least Uncle George had the decency not to put my face on any of them,' she said. She picked up an ink and wash monochrome drawing. 'This is the one I saw in Uncle George's studio.'

The Sergeant, who was showing signs of a much more delicate upbringing than I would have suspected, glanced round, flushed scarlet and looked up at the ceiling. 'You're sure?' she asked.

'Do you think I could be mistaken?' Beth retorted. She sounded amused.

Sergeant Bedale was back at the sink, dabbing away violently. She shook her head. 'But how can we be sure that Mr Muir or his widow didn't give them away?' she said.

'That's easy,' Beth said. 'I'll ask her.'

She left the room before I could stop her. I shuffled the drawings hastily back into their folder and waited for the explosion. Beth returned.

'I don't think Hattie knows about Uncle George's lady friends,' she said, 'so I just asked whether either of them had given any sketches to Mr Young. She said definitely not. She said that, after Uncle George was killed, Mr Young asked whether he could help himself to one or two sketches to remember his old friend by, but she wasn't giving anything away until the agent had been through them and advised her.'

'That does it,' the Sergeant said. But before she could get around to explaining exactly what it did, there was a loud scream from the garden.

Eight

We met Hattie in the hall. The four of us erupted onto the gravel together.

An electric cable snaked across the grass to where, across the drive from the patch of jungle, the road swung away and the hedge separated us from the adjacent field. Henry was lying on his back with the hedge-trimmer still in his hand and Isobel crouching over him. The cable, I noticed, had been severed close to the trimmer.

'Oh my God!' Isobel was saying over and over again.

Sergeant Bedale shouldered her aside and felt Henry's pulse. 'Ambulance,' she snapped. She put her hands over his heart and pressed sharply.

I raced back indoors and dialled the emergency services. When I returned to the scene, the Sergeant was administering the kiss of life. I thought, for a stupid moment, that it was a pity Henry wasn't awake to enjoy it. I also thought that the Sergeant, although as anxious as any of us, was secretly relieved to be called on for decisive action.

'An ambulance is on the way,' I said. 'They said that it wouldn't take long.'

'His heart had stopped,' Beth whispered. 'She says

that it's going again. I thought that she was going to bust his ribs.' She sounded awed by the nearness of death.

Isobel was wringing her hands. 'He ran the cable out for me,' she said, not for the first time. With another flash of insight, I thought that she was babbling just to give her mouth something to do instead of screaming again. 'He plugged the trimmer in and gave it a buzz to be sure that it was working, and he just went down in a heap. I thought he'd had a heart attack but when I touched him I felt a shock. He was still holding the trimmer and it was still running. I knew the first thing to do was to cut off the current, but it seemed miles back to the shed. So I just rammed the cable into the teeth of the trimmer.'

The Sergeant straightened her back. 'That was sensible,' she said. 'Best thing you could have done.' Henry made a snoring sound and breathed loudly.

Hattie had vanished. I saw her struggling back over the grass with an armful of blankets and went to help. We wrapped Henry against the chill of a day which was turning bitterly cold. His breathing faltered and Isobel turned white and swayed against Hattie. The Sergeant went back to work.

Beth pulled me aside. 'I thought that new thing you fitted— '

'The earth leakage circuit breaker?'

'Yes, that thing. I thought it was supposed to pop out and cut off the current if anything like that happened.'

'It is,' I said.

Henry was breathing again. Beth scuttled off across the grass. When she came back, she was grim-faced. 'The handle of the mower was leaning up against it,' she said. 'Who uses a lawn mower in the middle of winter?'

It seemed an odd question. 'Nobody,' I said.

'Exactly!'

An ambulance was coming through the village, flashing a blue light and braying uncertainly. I ran for the road and stood waving until they saw me and accelerated towards Three Oaks.

Two minutes later, Henry, now breathing steadily, had been lifted by stretcher into the ambulance. I had never seen Isobel, my calm, competent partner, so disoriented. She was determined to go with Henry in the ambulance and had little difficulty persuading Hattie to go with her for support.

Beth, the Sergeant and I were left standing aimlessly, like stragglers after a party.

I picked up the hedge-trimmer with its short, severed cord. 'I'll throw this away,' I said. 'It's time that we had one of the newer, plastic bodied ones.'

'No,' Beth said quickly. 'Save it. You might be throwing away evidence.'

'Of what?' I asked. I had had no time to think more deeply than of my anxiety over Henry.

She looked at me as though I were stupid. I was ashamed to recognise the look as one which I had thrown at her more than once over the years. 'Doesn't it seem to you that this was one accident too many?' she asked.

I suppose that I was still being slow, but too much had been happening. 'Who'd want to hurt Henry?' I asked. Beth started to coil up the cable. 'Be careful,' I said.

'I unplugged it at the other end. John, you're not thinking straight. Nobody wanted to hurt Henry. Who'd expect him to use the trimmer?'

'You, you mean?' Beth usually undertook all gardening work – Isobel assisting, against Beth's wishes, whenever she felt in need of fresh air and therapy. 'My God!' I said. 'Somebody tried to kill you?'

'Not me either,' Beth said patiently. 'Come into the house.'

'I'll take this apart,' I said. 'If somebody's tampered with the wiring— '

The Sergeant had been listening in rapt silence. 'In that event,' she said, 'you'd be destroying the evidence. The girl's right. Put it by.'

We trailed after Beth. I locked the trimmer away in my junk room and joined them in the kitchen. Beth had turned off the gasses, but the smell of Sunday lunch dominated the room. My watch said that lunch was already overdue and suddenly I realised that I was starving. When my uncertain appetite recovered it was inclined to do so with a bang.

'I'm ravenous,' I said.

'How can you think of food?' Beth began disgustedly. 'So'm I,' she added, and looked at Sergeant Bedale. 'You'll join us?'

The Sergeant nodded. 'While you tell me a bit more,' she said. Her clothes had picked up a whole lot more dog-dirt as she knelt over Henry, but she hadn't noticed.

'All right.' Beth looked at me, about to say something else, and took in my appearance for the first time. 'John, you're frozen.' She patted my clothes. 'And you're soaking wet. You've been hanging around out there without even a jacket on. You must be chilled through. Your lunch will keep a little longer. Go and take a hot bath and change your clothes.'

'Not if there's some nutter scattering accidents around and leaving them to happen,' I said.

'Nobody's in any danger just now,' Beth said in tones of exasperation. 'Except that you'll catch your death if you don't do what I say. Take my word for it. Go, go, go!'

Now that she mentioned it, I realised that my teeth were beginning to chatter. I was gripped by a chill which almost overrode my hunger. A hot bath followed by a meal and an explanation seemed a satisfactory programme.

As the water's heat slowly found its way deep into my bones, the old tiredness came over me. I must have dozed. My mind wandered in and around the recent events, rambling freely beyond the confines of time and geography. My dreams strayed into the realms of the incredible. Half waking, I told myself that I was beginning to fantasise. Fanta's eyes. It became a film title. *The Eyes of the Phanta.*

The water was suddenly cooler. I renewed its heat. Hunger and curiosity began to take over. I had been aware of female voices below me, pitched just at that maddening level where only the occasional word can be understood. Twice, the phone was used and once I heard it ring for an incoming call. Then, while I was hurriedly towelling myself and dressing in the luxury of clothes still warm from the airing cupboard, the sound of more discussion. The tones of voice ranged through petulant, persuasive, incredulous and assenting. Beth's voice and the Sergeant's were similar, so that I could only sometimes guess which was speaking.

Beth, despite her preoccupation with the Sergeant, must have followed my progress by the sound of doors and rushing water. As I came downstairs she was in the hall, holding a steaming plate but still speaking over her shoulder to the Sergeant in the kitchen.

'Use the bathroom, if you like,' she said.

'I can manage,' said Sergeant Bedale's voice.

'Would you like to borrow— '

'I'm all right,' said the Sergeant with irritation.

'Just finish giving it a good sponge, then, and dry it on the boiler.' The Sergeant's problem settled to her satisfaction, Beth smiled at me. 'You can eat this in the sitting room,' she said. 'We took ours on the trot but you're going to have a sit-down meal.'

Obediently, I carried the plate into the sitting room. The two Labradors were curled on the hearth-rug. Jason avoided my eye. He knew that he was not supposed to be in the house, but he was going to enjoy the fireside until somebody noticed and expelled him. I let it go. Beth followed me up with cutlery and poured me a glass of beer. 'I let Jason stay inside,' she said guiltily. 'He's upset.'

I had to sit awkwardly to eat off the low coffee table, but the slightly overdone roast chicken, mushy potatoes and cauliflower were worth the effort. Beth sat down nearby. 'Hattie phoned. Henry's out of danger. And you'd better hurry,' she added. 'We've a visitor coming.'

I waited until my mouth was more or less empty. 'Who?' I asked. 'No. Scrub that. First of all, if – and I'm not convinced yet – but if the trimmer was rigged to electrocute somebody, why not you? I could just about see your cousin knocking off first his uncle and then you, in the hope of getting his blasted tyke back.'

'Jason is not a blasted tyke,' Beth said firmly. 'He is a well pedigreed, highly intelligent and very beautiful Labrador. And Edgar wouldn't get him back that way.

He knew that Uncle George had left Jason to me and he also knew, because I told him . . . '

Her voice trailed away.

'Told him what?' I asked.

Beth looked down at her fingers. 'That I'd made a will on one of those form things, leaving you everything.'

'Everything?' I said. 'Golly gee!'

I had intended to speak lightly, but sarcasm crept through my embarrassment and into my voice. She pulled a face at me. 'Apart from Jason, I know that there's not much more than a few pairs of knickers and some wellies and you couldn't get into them. Not the wellies, anyway. But when I inherited the picture and Hattie gave me the ring I realised that I was suddenly a woman of property and that I should do something about it.'

I felt ashamed. I had never thought to make out my own will. 'Thank you,' I said gently. 'That was very thoughtful.'

She looked at her watch. 'He'll be here in a minute. Listen, John. If we can, we're to handle this and to leave Gillian out of it— '

'Mm?' My mouth was full again.

'Sergeant Bedale. She asked me to call her Gillian. She's in a rather nervous state, poor thing. On tenterhooks, sort of. She daren't get herself in any deeper, she's already gone out on a limb up to her neck.'

I managed to extract a meaning from the confusion of metaphors and swallowed hastily in order to voice my indignation. 'You mean that she'll be happy to make an arrest if you – we – can incriminate a murderer for her?' I paused and found that I had to laugh. 'Nervous state? That woman has the nerve of the devil. She comes here ordering me around like some sort of supercilious aunt. When the going gets tough, she flutters her eyelashes and gets out the soft soap. Now, when she's really landed herself in it, she wants to keep her head down and let us do all the work while she grabs any credit that's going.'

'That's about it,' Beth answered cheerfully. 'I said that we'd do it. Somebody has to do something.'

Thinking it over, I decided that we owed the Sergeant a favour for saving Henry's life. 'But do what?' I said. 'Start from the beginning. Who was meant to be electrocuted?'

'That isn't the beginning. It's almost the end. All right,' she said as she saw that I was trying to clear my mouth again. 'Isobel, of course.'

I tried to wash my mouthful down with beer and nearly choked. Before I could find my voice again, tyres crunched in the drive and Beth said, 'Ah, here he is. You stay here. I'll get him to put his car in the barn. It wouldn't do if it were to be seen, would it?'

I shook my head. It seemed easier to agree than to ask why some unspecified person's car should not be seen outside our door.

As I finished working my way through my meal, I was also chewing on Beth's words. I even began to make some sort of sense of them, to the point of not being taken altogether by surprise when the visitor turned out to be our Texan friend, Ken Boyce. He had exchanged his smart tweeds of the day before for a thin business suit, barely warm enough for a Scottish winter.

Beth grabbed up my empty plate and went through to the kitchen, leaving me to attend to the courtesies. I offered him the most comfortable chair, he refused a drink and we sat looking at each other.

'That,' Mr Boyce said at last, 'is a very remarkable young lady. Just what the hell is she up to?'

'She is,' I said, 'and I'm damned if I know. Your guess is as good as mine. Probably better, because you know what she said to you and I don't know even that.'

'She just called up and asked me to get my ass over here – not in so many words, you understand. She was polite, but there was only one answer she was going to accept, and by God it wasn't going to be "No"! The rest of what she said, well, it went right by me.'

I nodded sympathetically. 'She can get a bit obscure when she's excited,' I said.

'That's for sure.'

Beth came back with a plate of Hattie's apple pie for me and coffee all round. She made another trip and fetched the package of George Muir's drawings, which she laid unopened on the table.

'Now,' I said, 'You'd better explain, slowly and clearly, to both of us, just what the hell you're up to.'

'All right,' Beth said. She looked steadily at Mr Boyce with her spaniel's eyes and I could see his slight irritation melting away. Beth's eyes had that effect on people – especially men. 'My uncle – George Muir, the painter – was killed in his studio in what the police at first accepted as an accident. He was hand-loading some shotgun cartridges and his pot of powder blew up in his face.'

Ken Boyce nodded. 'I read an obituary,' he said. 'I wondered. I do some loading myself and I had trouble believing that accident. A Class B propellant burns kind of slow, unless it's confined long enough to get going.'

'It was a heavy pot,' I said, 'with a very tight-fitting lid. To judge from the other pot, the one he kept his shot in, you had to jerk hard to get the lid off.'

'I guess that could do it,' Boyce said.

Beth took up the tale again. 'John was curious. He noticed that a tiny hole had been drilled in the pot. And there were one or two other things, such as there being some pellets of shot in with the remains of the powder. After putting two and two together and coming up with an answer as near to four as makes no difference, he decided that he had doubts and that he ought to let the police know.

'We don't have inquests in Scotland. The police just report to the procurator fiscal, who decides whether there should be an inquiry in front of the sheriff. In my uncle's case, they'd already decided that it was an accident, so the police weren't exactly falling over themselves to re-open it. They sent a woman detective sergeant to look into the evidence. They probably hinted that she should go away for a couple of days and then report back that it was an accident right enough.

'Either she's conscientious or John was convincing, or maybe both. She decided that more investigation was needed. So far so good. But she went off at half-cock, got a search warrant and searched a house.'

Ken Boyce understood. 'So now she's got to make good or back off?'

'It's worse than that. She'd been told to handle it with kid gloves. When her bosses get back to work tomorrow morning, she'd better have something to back herself up. The pity is that she searched the wrong house and the owner's not going to be satisfied with anything less than her head on a plate.'

'The ultimate sin,' Boyce said. 'Being wrong.'

'But she did find something,' Beth said. 'What she came up with isn't direct evidence and yet it could be vital.

'Then, just a couple of hours ago, Mr Kitts had an accident. His wife, Isobel, is a partner in the kennels. He was nearly electrocuted by a hedge-trimmer. I'm sure the experts will find that the wiring had been tampered with – '

'I doubt it,' I broke in. 'Any fool could loosen a wire and leave it pressed against the metal handle. You could never prove that it hadn't happened in the course of being bumped around.'

'All right.' Beth said, with irritation. 'But the safety device in the shed had been nullified by having the handle of the lawn mower leant against it. Again, it could have happened through carelessness. But it was becoming obvious that too many accidents were happening around here.'

Ken Boyce held up a hand to stop her while he took time for thought. Beth waited patiently. 'I see who you're getting at,' he said at last. 'And it's right that I should know. But before we go into the matter of just how the hell he could have fixed it from way across the Atlantic, can you tell me why?'

'You may be able to tell us,' Beth said. 'Mr Boyce, tell me something else first. Are you easily shocked?'

Ken Boyce's eyebrows shot straight up his forehead. He half smiled. 'Why no, ma'am,' he said. 'I guess not. I'd say that I was the least shockable person you'll ever meet.'

'I hope that's true. My uncle was a lady's man, Mr Boyce. I've known it since I was a child, although I've only recently come to realise what an amorous old rascal he really was. And, being first and foremost an artist, he didn't make diary notes or take photographs or collect little souvenirs. He kept a different sort of reminder. Don't judge him too harshly. I don't think that any of them were meant to be seen by anybody other than himself and perhaps that particular lady. Perhaps you can recognise somebody.'

She opened the folder.

Ken Boyce leafed through the drawings. His face was impassive except that his eyebrows seemed to have disappeared altogether. 'It's a pity that he never signed these,' he said. 'They'd bring a mint from the right sort of collector. As it is, you tell your aunt, if they're still her property, that I know men back in the States who'd pay good money for— '

He stopped dead. He was holding a water-colour sketch, in full colour, of a chubby blonde. She was wearing a necklace and earrings, long gloves and one stocking, and she seemed highly amused at being sketched in that state. The drawing had been carried out with a minimum of strokes and colours and yet it was almost magically alive. The artist had even caught the soft glow which a woman diffuses after love.

'Mrs Fullerton?' Beth asked.

'The second Mrs Fullerton,' Boyce confirmed.

Something in his tone gave me the hint. 'You didn't exactly throw up your hands in horror at the suggestion that Bruce Fullerton might be arranging accidents,' I said. 'Does the reason why you aren't surprised have anything to do with the first Mrs Fullerton?'

'That's right,' Boyce said sadly. He dropped the sketches on the table and leaned back in his chair. 'I've known Bruce Fullerton for around twenty years. He was an engineer before he moved across into marketing and came home to Scotland. Worked for the firm back in the States. I remember his first wife well. A good-looking woman, but she had two problems. One was drinking and the other was messing around. You know what I mean? She liked men, any men. The marriage had been on the rocks for years. I reckoned it only lasted as long as it did because she'd brought some money into it with her.

'Then, while Bruce was on the West Coast, solving a problem at our Californian plant, they found his wife lying dead. When she was alone and more or less sober, she used to do the gardening. She had a great touch with flowers, although sometimes she used to get stoned out of her mind and pull up her best plants in mistake for weeds. They figured that she'd mixed some weedkiller and put the left-over into an empty whisky bottle. Then, one day, when she was good and plastered, she forgot and drank from the same bottle. That's what they figured.'

'And you?' I said. 'What did you figure?'

'Me? I figured that it'd be easy to fill a spare bottle with weedkiller and leave her to get around to it. None of my business, and if that's what he'd done I couldn't hardly blame him. Might've done the same myself, if I'd been stuck with a wife like that. And if I'd had the guts.

'No, I'm not surprised – except that it seemed to me he'd struck luckier, second time around. What d'you reckon's been happening over this side?'

'That's the big question,' Beth said. 'There are still some things we don't know for sure. I'll try to put it in order, John can help me and maybe you can fill in some gaps.

'Mr Fullerton told John that he and his wife met my uncle for the first time in some hotel. The Fullertons were there for dinner, but my uncle was with a woman and they'd booked in for the night. John?'

My mind had been racing ahead. I came back with a start. 'The way Fullerton described Mr Muir's companion, he made her sound remarkably like his own wife – to judge from that sketch. Of course, there's more than one plump blonde around . . . '

'God has been good to us,' Boyce agreed, smiling.

' . . . but Fullerton may have had a good reason to substitute his wife's desccription. The last thing he needed was for Muir's connection with Mrs Fullerton to become public knowledge. If somebody had seen my fiancée's uncle with Mrs Fullerton and had described her to me, I'd never have connected the two after that piece of misdirection.' As I spoke, another connection jumped into my mind. 'When I asked Fullerton the name of the hotel, he visibly jumped.

'Anyway, Fullerton told me that he recognised George Muir and asked him to do a portrait of his dog. He took the dog to Muir's studio for a sitting when Mrs Muir was out, so that's probably when he found out that the key was usually left above the door. He told me that the dog had come to him from his late sister and meant a lot to him.'

'That sure does sound like Bruce,' Ken Boyce said. 'He always was a sucker for a dog. I remember him getting into a fight in New Jersey once when a big trucker gave his dog a push with his foot, a mutt you wouldn't have given doodlysquat for. But maybe he had the right way of it. Seems like he got more fidelity from his dogs than he ever got from his women. Go ahead.'

'Then it was time for him to spend some time in America,' Beth said, 'learning the details of all the new products.'

'If Uncle George had been taken with Mrs Fullerton when they met, it would be easy for him to pay her a visit on the excuse that he wanted to make some more sketches of the dog. And an affair started. I'm told,' Beth said distantly, 'that my uncle had a sort of old world charm which had the ladies falling over him. I couldn't see it myself.'

'You wouldn't,' Boyce said. 'That approach doesn't work with young singles; but I've seen married women, whose husbands have forgotten about the little courtesies, fall for it every time.

'I never knew who the other party was, but from the phone calls Bruce was getting and from what he said, I gathered that another marriage was going down the tube. I didn't pay it much heed. I'd met his second wife on my previous trip and it seemed to me that they were very much in love. But honeymoons don't last for ever. We don't look on marriage as any too permanent back home, not the way you do here. Hell, I've been married three times myself. You know what they say – a change being as good as a rest. But Bruce sure did seem to be getting uptight about it.

'When he went off for the weekend by himself, I was more relieved than anything. I'd had him around for weeks and he was becoming a pain in the ass, if you'll pardon the expression, and I was glad of the chance of a get-together with the lady who'll be Wife Number Four if I get over my present indisposition towards the wedded state. I thought nothing of it.'

'Not even when your passport went missing?' I asked suddenly. 'It didn't strike me at the time, but there's a similarity between the two of you.'

Boyce looked at me as if I had offered an insult. 'You don't say that?'

'You're younger and better looking than he is,'

Beth said quickly. As far as I could remember, she had never set eyes on Fullerton. 'But there's enough resemblance that, if he smudged your passport photograph a bit and let his stubble come in, a passport control office would put any difference down to jet lag . . . '

'Now that never did strike me,' Boyce said. He seemed amused by Beth's flattery. 'I'm a mite taller than he is but I guess our faces are much the same shape. I never looked for the passport until I came to need it, and then it could have been in my luggage or in the office or at home. I thought at the time that it had been mislaid. You think he took it?'

'That's the way it looks,' Beth said. 'He wouldn't want a record of his own passport being used. And he couldn't put it back because it would have been stamped with a visit to Britain you'd never made.'

'Looks,' Boyce said. 'Would. Could. Seems to me that there's a lot of guessing going around.'

'If you think that what we've said so far included a lot of guesswork,' Beth said, 'just wait! He may have come back to try for a reconciliation, but if – yes, I know, another if – if he borrowed a passport and told his colleagues that he was going skiing, it suggests that, at the very least, the death of his wife was on the cards. He'd been hurt once and now it was happening again.

'I think that he flew over, on your passport. He hired another car and went home. His wife died, perhaps by premeditated murder or perhaps in a furious quarrel. He arranged it to look as if she'd slipped and fallen downstairs. He was in a highly emotional state . . . '

'He's an emotional guy,' Boyce said. 'Always was.'

' . . . and my uncle was the man who'd come between

himself and his happy, second marriage. Arranging accidents was becoming a habit. He drove over to Tarbet and waited his chance when the house was empty. He'd already seen the studio and he knew about Uncle George's loading— '

'Now hold on just a minute,' I said. 'We've been thinking about fuses and timers and remote controls and things. But he was going back to New York and he couldn't hang around and wait for your uncle to start a reloading session. He'd have had to catch Sunday's plane at the latest.'

'If you'll stop jumping to conclusions we'll get on quicker,' Beth said severely. (Boyce shot me a look and tried to hide a grin.) 'I never liked any of the complicated ideas you came up with. I don't know much about these things. I'd be no good as a terrorist's do-it-yourself bomb-maker. I'm a simple soul and I was thinking along simpler lines.'

'Simple ideas are often the best,' Ken Boyce said.

'Thank you. Uncle George was going to get around to his reloading some day, and Mr Fullerton left a trap waiting for that day. There was no hurry. Revenge can wait. Perhaps it's all the better in prospect, I wouldn't know. I'm not the vengeful type. I expect that he improvised something from what he knew was already available on the spot.'

'That sounds like him,' Boyce said. 'Bruce always had a quick mind. When he was an engineer and a problem came up, he'd have it analysed and a solution improvised before the rest of us had appreciated the problem.'

Beth looked at me. 'John, didn't you say something about a fishing reel in the top drawer under the work-bench?'

'Two reels,' I said.

'I remember those reels. They were on a shelf over the door when I saw them last spring. Was there a nail or a drawing-pin or something?'

'Yes there was,' I said. 'There was a drawing-pin stuck in the bottom of the drawer. The end of one of the fishing lines was tied to it. I decided he'd used it to anchor the end of the line while he wound it onto the reel.'

'That doesn't sound right,' Boyce said. 'That isn't the way you do it. You wind the line straight onto the reel from the spool you bought in the store.'

'Was the very end of the line tied to the pin?' Beth asked me. 'Or was there a tail left?'

I called up a mental picture. 'There was a tail,' I said. 'Not very much. Maybe a couple of feet, curled up beside the pin. Why?'

'This is how I see it,' Beth said. 'The fishing reels were on the shelf. He took them down and put them in the drawer just as a reason for there to be some thin fishing line around. He used Uncle George's tools to drill a tiny hole in the pot and he took the end of the fishing line up the back of the bench and passed it through the hole. He tied a match-head on the end and glued a piece of sandpaper onto the bottom of the pot.'

'Jesus H Christ!' Boyce exclaimed. I think that I was too stunned by Beth's lethal ingenuity to say anything.

'He'd need something to press the match-head down,' Beth went on, 'and I think he used some of the lead shot in a twist of thin paper. Then he topped the pot up with Uncle George's explosive shotgun powder.'

I came out of my trance. 'No. He brought his own. Your uncle's was a slow, progressive powder. He'd need something altogether faster.'

'Pistol powder,' Boyce said firmly. 'That has to be fast enough to burn up before the bullet's gone more than a few inches. Hell, you can wreck a rifle, using pistol powder.'

'If you say so.' Beth paused to recover her original train of thought after what had been, to her, an irrelevant digression. 'The first time Uncle George pulled open the drawer or pulled forward his pot of powder, the match-head would scrape over the sandpaper and . . . '

'Bang?' said Boyce.

'Just that. The paper would mostly burn and blow away, the shot would be scattered and the end of the nylon fishing line would melt. The rest of the line would take up its natural curl and coil itself down beside the drawing-pin.'

'That would work,' Boyce said slowly. 'By Christ it would work! If I marry again, I'll never do hand-loading without having a very gentle feel around for any bits of thin fishing line. That stuff's the next thing to invisible. But it seems to me, young lady, you've shown us how something could have been done, which is a hell of a way from proving that it was done.'

'I think that it must have been done that way,' I said. 'It fits exactly what I saw in the studio and explains a whole lot of anomalies which had me puzzled. But that's not to say that it was done by Bruce Fullerton. He looks guilty, but we don't know that he took Ken's passport. And ladies do sometimes fall downstairs in empty houses.'

'Of course,' Beth said impatiently. 'That's the whole problem. A man going around arranging accidents and being miles away when they happen needn't leave a whole lot of proof behind. By the time there's any investigation, the evidence has all been lost or covered up. Even if the wiring in the hedge-trimmer has been tampered with— '

'It'll probably turn out to be a loose wire,' I pointed out again.

'And nothing to show whether anybody loosened it,' Ken Boyce added.

'And,' I added, 'What has Isobel to do with it anyway?'

'I was just coming to that,' Beth snapped. 'if you two will just shut up for a moment and stop jumping about and repeating yourselves. Just accept, for one credulous moment, that Mr Fullerton did what I say he did. He must have left a whole trail of evidence behind which a proper investigation by detectives and forensic scientists would uncover, but unless Sergeant Bedale takes a strong case to her superiors, that investigation may never happen.

'Now we'll come back to Isobel. After everything was done the way we've said, he would still have had to deal with one loose end. He couldn't just leave his favourite dog there with his wife's body.'

'Why not?' I asked.

'I can tell you that,' Boyce said. 'Their house is way out in the sticks. No regular help, no nothing. When she wanted some help about the place there was a woman she called in, and the same for help in the garden. Rest of the time, she was on her own. If she wanted company, she went out for it. She could have lain there and nobody found her until the dog had starved.'

'Right,' Beth said. 'So he put the dog into kennels. He couldn't do it as himself. But he's small for a man and quite slim. He put on his wife's coat and some make-up and a hat and went, after dark, to the one kennels whose owners – the Springs – are notoriously short-sighted and absent-minded. It was his bad luck that Isobel happened to be there at the time and accepted the dog from him – or, at least, from somebody who she described afterwards as a very odd-looking woman with a husky voice. Mr Fullerton had been a client of hers, years ago, when she was working as a vet. And then, yesterday, he saw her looking at him and knew that she might be making the connection.

'He must have come up here last night and had a good look around. He noticed that the hedge was only trimmed halfway along and he picked on the hedge-trimmer as a suitable weapon. The garden shed's never locked. You remember who saw Isobel using the hedge-trimmer the other day?'

I was still warm from my bath but I felt a deep chill. Beth could so easily have been the innocent bystander who stopped the wrong bullet. 'Fullerton did,' I said. 'And he pulled forward, out of her sight, before he got out of the car. That clinches it as far as I'm concerned.'

'Well, as far as the law's concerned,' Beth said scornfully, 'it won't do anything of the sort. If there was any tampering with the trimmer, which we may not be able to prove, it could have been by somebody who'd seen me using it and had some reason we don't know about to want me out of the way.'

Part of my mind had been sifting the facts and suppositions and trying to arrive at a possible timetable. 'What about the dates?' I asked. 'Do they fit?'

'They could,' Beth said. 'Isobel said that the setter was brought to the Springs' kennels on the Saturday evening that one of our bitches went down with mastitis. I've looked in the kennel diary and that was four weeks ago yesterday.'

Boyce fished in a waistcoat pocket and pulled out a small diary. 'That's the weekend that Bruce went skiing. They phoned him a few days later. From the body and other signs, his wife had her fall the previous Saturday.'

Beth nodded energetically. 'Gillian phoned a friend – a former boyfriend, I think – in the Fife CID and he looked it up for her. That's what the report said.'

'And he flew back immediately?' I asked.

'Within a few days,' Boyce said.

'Then,' I said, 'he took a hell of a time getting round to asking about the portrait and mentioning the dog. He seemed to imply that he'd only just arrived back in this country. If his wife had collected the portrait, why did he . . . ?' The answer hit me while I was still asking the question. 'He span the tale about his wife and the dog to explain the dog's absence. He had to keep the dog out of sight for a while to give it time to forget, because the dog had seen him kill his wife. When I saw them together in the car, the setter was in a very nervous state, not like a dog which had just been restored to a beloved owner. His own dog was a witness against him.'

'Wild guesswork,' Beth complained.

'It may be all of that,' Ken Boyce said. 'But John here goes along with your belief that your uncle's accident was rigged and he seems to know what he's talking about. And that point about the dog's a clincher. Folk would soon have started talking if they'd seen his own dog cowering away from him, just after his wife was killed.

'I know Bruce Fullerton. I may not have been meeting him face to face for all that time, but we've worked together for years and it's crazy how you can get to know somebody, even someone who you've never met, if you exchange enough correspondence and phone calls. After a while, you can guess just how they'll react. Bruce is nervous, impetuous, ruthless, ingenious, vengeful – and he's slippery. He has a knack of making sure that he never carries the can. Hell, you've just about painted his portrait more clearly than your uncle could have done it.

'To me, as somebody who knows him and his character and his history, you've connected up all the known facts, right down to things like my missing passport, in a way that carries conviction. It might not stand up in a court of law, but it sure as hell stands up with me because that's just the way he'd have acted.' Boyce hesitated and made a gesture of unease. 'As you said, your police would be able to uncover a whole lot more evidence if they set their minds to it, but you say you don't have enough to make them re-open the case of your uncle. Or of either of the Mrs Fullertons?'

'Not yet,' Beth said. 'I talked it over with Sergeant Bedale – while you were in the bath, John, and before we phoned you, Mr Boyce. She feels that if she hasn't anything more solid by tomorrow morning she'll be called off and given a black mark and Mr Fullerton will be safe for ever. Until somebody else offends him or he decides to have another go at Isobel or something.'

I felt the cold shivers on my back again. Somebody out there might be deciding that I knew too much and be preparing to cut the car's brake-pipes or electrify the wire mesh of the runs. And Beth might as easily fall the victim. 'What can we do?' I asked.

'Gillian and I discussed that. We decided that the only hope would be to make him commit himself, one way or the other. She spoke to the Fife Police. Her old friend, a detective sergeant like herself, was on duty. He's gone to watch the house and he'll report by radio.' Beth produced a sheet of paper half covered with her clear, round writing. 'If you could ring him up, Mr Boyce, and make some excuse for phoning, and tell him something like this, but in your own words . . . '

Boyce ran his eye quickly over the page. 'Hell, I don't need any excuse,' he said. 'This is made to measure. I was supposed to join him for a drink around five, for a few, final words before I go to catch my plane tomorrow.'

The extension telephone was on a long enough cord to reach him where he sat. He dialled a number from memory and sat waiting, his brow puckered in thought. He stiffened suddenly.

'Bruce?' he said. 'This is Ken. I find I can't come over this evening. The local fuzz called me up a few minutes back . . . Sure, I'll still come over if I get away in good time, but I think we've covered all the main subjects. I can phone you if anything else comes up . . . Nope, nothing to get in an uproar about. They want to meet me at Three Oaks Kennels around five. Something about that lady I went around with, last time I was over here. Seems there's some pictures there and they want to know do I recognise anybody . . . No, not photographs, they said something about drawings by some man called Muir. His widow's there now . . . Yeah, sounds crazy, but I can only tell you as much as I know. Listen, in case I don't make it this evening, thanks for looking after me while I've been over here. We'll be in touch.'

He hung up and looked at the two of us in turn. 'I sure hope we're wrong,' he said.

'I'll go and tell Gillian,' Beth said. She left the room.

'One thing I don't get,' Ken Boyce said to me. 'Surely he'd have checked whether there was a sketch of his old lady while he was in the studio fixing up for the explosion?'

It was a good point and it took me a few seconds to think of the answer. 'He probably did check,' I said. 'But he may have expected a fire to follow the explosion. In the meantime, if George Muir had noticed that one particular sketch had gone missing, he'd have realised that there'd been an intruder and he might have looked around enough to spot other things out of place.'

Boyce was nodding steadily. 'You may have been partly wrong about his motivation in visiting Tarbet, the time you met him over there. Mrs Fullerton had already collected the dog's portrait for him, but when he heard that there hadn't been a fire he went to Mrs Muir's house anyway and span his tale so that he could ask for his photographs back and any sketches.'

'You're right,' I said. 'That gave him a chance to look through the pile. It must have given him a jolt when he didn't find them there. A neighbour had already helped himself.'

Beth came back. She was carrying a small, police-type radio which she placed carefully on the coffee table. It was hissing softly. 'Gillian gave me this. She can justify asking for Mr Fullerton's house to be watched, but if anything goes wrong or if the whole thing's a frost, she wants to be able to say that she knew nothing about it.'

'She wants jam on both sides,' I said, 'and no bread in the middle.'

'Which of us doesn't? And now,' Beth said, 'there's nothing to do but wait.'

'You may not have to wait long.' Boyce said. 'Bruce was always a quick thinker and he'll have to move fast. He thinks that the police are going to be here by five – and he's only got a few miles to come.'

Nine

So far, I had been swept along by the decisions of others. Now, given time to think, I found that my mind was a jumble of conflicting logic. If the others were right, something was far wrong. But if I was right they were wrong and everything was all right. I went back to the beginning and started again. If . . .

The radio squawked suddenly. 'He's leaving the house,' it said. 'Entering car.'

'He won't come here,' I said. 'It's too obviously a trap. He'll run for it, using your passport.'

'You want to bet on that?' Boyce asked me.

'I'm not a betting man.' Especially, I could have added, against Texans who, when they bet, bet big.

'Just as well. We know it's a trap. But it's indirect enough to be convincing.'

'He's reached the main road. Turning north,' said the radio.

'Towards us,' Beth said.

'And towards several mainline stations and the airstrip,' I said. 'For all I know, it's also towards his lady friend.'

Ken Boyce leaned back comfortably in his chair. 'Look at it from his viewpoint,' he said. 'Bruce

Fullerton's worst fault, if you don't count the accidents that seem to happen to folk he doesn't like when he isn't around any more, has always been that he's impetuous and over-confident.

'In the bind that he's in now he believes that, whether he sits tight or makes a run for it, in not many minutes I'll be saying, "Hey! That looks mighty like the late Mrs Fullerton the Second, who died of an accident much like the one which carried off Mrs Fullerton the First," and you'll say, "Would that be any connection with the Fullerton who seemed to be a steady visitor at George Muir's house, just before and after he was killed in another accident?" and then, given a jump-lead start and an hour or two to think it over, some copper's brain's going to start making connections. Next day, they'll be showing his photograph around the car-hire firms and asking the police back home whether he really went skiing in Vermont. Either way, he's a dead duck.

'On the other hand, if he can get in and out, wiping out the evidence before the cops arrive, they may think it smells as fishy as a beached whale, but they'll have no reason to sniff at him more than at anybody else.'

While Boyce was speaking in his slow drawl, I followed the occasional reports on the radio. Knowing the district well, it was easy to picture the progress of the big BMW. As it neared the turnoff for the village, I found that I was holding my breath. If it went straight on, Fullerton was on the run. Or else he was on some perfectly innocent errand . . .

'Turning left,' the radio said.

When Beth had first proposed the setting of a trap, I had had a vague and comfortable vision of Fullerton being arrested at our gates, or arriving at our front door to attempt some hopeless bluff. But, now that I had time to think about it, Fullerton's style was more for swift, covert but ruthless action.

Beth was the picture of patient expectation. I caught her eye. 'What do you think happens now? What does he do? What do we do?'

For the first time in an hour, she looked uncertain. 'He commits himself,' she said, 'and the police take him away. We watch. We'll be witnesses.'

'Did you and the Sergeant think this through before gambling with our lives?' I asked her. My mouth was dry. 'He's not going to prepare a trap which might not be sprung for days or weeks. If Ken's right, he needs instant results. And if you're right, he spent part of last night exploring the place. Some plan will already be maturing in his mind. And we're not ready for him.'

'He pulled into the carpark of the pub,' the radio said. 'Seems to have vanished. My mate's gone inside to see what he's up to.'

The pub? Did he need bracing for what was to come? Or was he going to phone for an appointment?

'He wouldn't drive up to the house,' Boyce said quietly. 'My bet is, he'll be walking from there.'

'You're right,' I said. I put out my hand for the radio but it spoke before I reached it. 'He isn't inside.'

I picked up the radio and found the TRANSMIT button. 'There's a double hedge and sunken track starts one field behind the pub and leads almost to the back of the kennels,' I said. 'He'll be coming that way. You haven't a hope of following him along there in daylight. You'd better come up here quickly, on foot.'

'Who's that?' the radio enquired suspiciously.
'I'm speaking for Sergeant Bedale.'
'And where's "here"?'
'Follow the road out of the village. At the first bend there's a gateway to a house on the left. Come straight to the house or you'll set the dogs barking and warn him off.'
The radio sighed, dispiritedly. 'It's started to snow,' it said and then fell silent.
'What's he going to do?' Beth asked in a whisper.
'I wish you'd wondered about that before rushing into this thing,' I said peevishly. 'I don't know what he's got in mind.'
'The police— '
'Won't be much use if he arrives with a stick of dynamite in his hand,' I pointed out.
'He won't, will he?' Beth's face looked pinched.
Fullerton had been at home when Boyce phoned him. So he probably thought that his electrical trap had not yet taken effect. He would expect Isobel to be with us, perhaps going over her records as was her Sunday habit. Or she might be at her home, in which case he could pay a later visit.
I got to my feet and stood, dithering. It seemed to me that nothing much short of a bomb would answer Fullerton's present problem. He had hardly had time to fabricate such a thing; and nothing that I could think of suggested that he might already have made one for some other emergency. Was he carrying a can of petrol? Another tin of pistol powder? If I looked, I might see.
The farmhouse had been built on a south-facing slope with a fair view in that direction. Whoever designed the house had determined to make the most of the view and the sunshine. Every possible window

faced south. In the north face of the building were only the two small windows of the office and my junk room and the bathroom skylight.

I hurried through into the office, squeezed between the desk and the filing cabinets and stooped to the window which was only partly obstructed by Isobel's box-files of computer disks.

It was staring me in the face. It even looked like a white-painted bomb. If it had not become such a familiar part of the scenery I would have thought of it sooner.

When we acquired Three Oaks, the heating and cooking had been by low pressure, liquid gas. This, I suppose, had also served such equipment as a grain drier. The cylindrical tank which held the liquid gas had been in one of the old farm sheds, now removed. It stood in the open on its brick piers. It had been refilled by tanker only ten days earlier.

My mind zigzagged around the possibilities.

A tracer bullet from a distance would send it up, but I thought that it would fireball on the spot, doing little more damage than to scorch the back of the house. And Fullerton would be unlikely to have access to any such exclusively military ammunition.

But when the sheds had been removed and the land graded and grassed, before I had even moved into the house, a dip had been left. It was only a shallow depression, but on such a breathless day it would channel any leakage of the heavier-than-air gas towards the back wall of the house, to find its way through the subfloor ventilators into the underbuilding. This possibility had worried me at the time; I was in no doubt about the explosive qualities of LPG when mixed with air. At the time, the North Sea Gas mains were being brought ever nearer, month by month. Rather than convert to oil or undertake more earth-moving, I had checked that the pipework was sound and had then invested in a cheap, automatic gas-detector. Unfortunately, the gas main had still not progressed closer than the village and the huge cylinder was still in use.

Fullerton need only break the seal on the drainage cock which permitted occasional cleaning out of condensate. If he left the gas to escape, he could expect it to build up rapidly beneath the house. He could then choose between hanging around to furnish ignition from a safe distance, or making tracks and being well out of harm's way before the gas found a naked light. Fuelled by the gas, a fire would be sure to follow the explosion.

Time was slipping away. I took one last look at the outside world. The sky was slate-grey although the daylight was ghostly pale. The first snowflakes of winter were already dappling the dark ground in random patches. A black figure crossed a gap in a dry stone wall, less than fifty yards away.

I bolted back towards the hall and slammed into Beth. I held her until she got her breath back. She made a confused sound of interrogation.

'No time to explain,' I said. 'Go and open doors and windows. Front of the house only. Got it?'

She nodded and turned away.

I dived into the cupboard under the stairs where both the meters were housed, pulled the main electricity switch and turned off the gas valve. That should shut off all pilot lights and prevent any thermostatic switches from producing sparks as they did their well-meaning duty.

That only left the gas-detector which hung in the hall. It had its own batteries. It was supposed to be sealed against gas, but Fate, I thought, might fancy the poetic irony of a spark from the gas-detector setting off the explosion, and subsequent blaze. I switched it off.

Beth had opened the front door and moved on. Something dark showed against the snowflakes. I went to the door. Two men came panting over the gravel.

'He's just arriving at the back of the house,' I said, keeping my voice low. 'I think he means to open the cock on the gas tank. If he does, he's virtually admitting to two murders and another attempt. Nail him.' The men separated in opposite directions. 'And for God's sake turn the gas off again.'

Beth and Boyce joined me in the hall. 'That sounds real mean,' Ken said. 'There was a school blew up that way in New London, years back. More'n two hundred children were killed.' I noticed that his face was pale, showing up a faint stubble.

Beth took my hand and squeezed it. 'We heard what you said,' she told me. 'What do we do?'

'You get the hell out of here,' I said 'Ken . . . '

'Yep.' Ken grabbed Beth's wrist and set off towards the road. Beth looked back at me and held out a hand in appeal. I think that she was going to scream at me to be careful or to come with them, but I put my finger to my lips. To her great credit, she nodded and let Ken Boyce pull her away. I turned back into the house.

There was no smell of gas as yet. It was cold in the hall with the door open and the heating off. While I wondered what remained to be done, I might be better off in the sitting room where at least there was . . . I remembered suddenly that the fire was still burning. God! Would I never get anything right?

And the two dogs were in front of the fire.

And the Sergeant was in the kitchen.

The army had trained me to stay calm and to use reason in an emergency; but reason, I found, went out of the window when my own treasures were at risk. I tried frantically to select the most certain way of extinguishing a log fire in a hurry. Even a bucket of water would not get to the heart of a glowing log. And while I struggled with that puzzle I was also competing against myself in a mental version of the old game – Who or What Would You Save First From a Fire?

Still no smell of gas, but would I smell it in the hall by the time that the first gas reached the hearth and led flame back to the gas below the floor?

Whistle for the dogs, shout to the Sergeant and I might have time to grab the Dickson before I ran after Beth. I tried to whistle and to shout, but I tried to do both at the same time and the only result was an extraordinary noise which was properly ignored.

There were other noises outside. Three figures appeared with a suddenness that made me jump. Fullerton, his hands cuffed behind his back, was dwarfed between the two policemen. His lips were clamped shut as though he was determined never to say another word, but the glare in his eyes was hot enough to have triggered a gas explosion.

'He turned your gas on,' one of the policemen said. 'It's off again. You want to make a statement now?'

I leaned against the doorpost and took several deep breaths while the panic ebbed out of me. 'Any time you like,' I said.

The other officer was looking around him. 'Where's Sergeant Bedale?' he asked. 'What we've got mightn't stand up in court on its own. If she's been the investigating officer in a larger enquiry, she should make the actual arrest. I understand there's at least one other charge to be brought later.'

'Two,' I said. 'Possibly three. Maybe four. You'd better come in.'

They led Fullerton into the house. I opened the kitchen door for them.

Beth and Isobel later accused me of doing it out of spite, because Sergeant Bedale had irked me during our earlier encounters. But I had honestly forgotten what had befallen the Sergeant.

And that is how it happened that Bruce Fullerton was arrested for murder by a scarlet-faced police sergeant clad only in a fetching pair of pink silk camiknickers. It was a scene to which only the pencil of the late George Muir could have done justice.

By the time that the officers had taken preliminary statements and removed their prisoner to temporary accommodation in Cupar, we were running very late and the dogs were leaving us in no doubt that they were dying of hunger pangs. Beth, assisted by Ken Boyce, prepared their evening meal while I set about relighting the pilot lights and setting time-clocks. Life has to go on.

In the middle of it all, the phone rang. I took the call in the kitchen, glad of an excuse to sit down. It was Hattie again, her usual composed self. Henry was conscious and would probably be home in a few days. Until then, she would stay with Isobel rather than abandon her to an empty house. And, she enquired, had there been any new developments?

The news would be public property within a few hours, but it was too long a story to tell over the phone. I told her that Bruce Fullerton had been arrested and that he would probably be charged with the murder of her husband.

There was silence on the line. 'It was on account of one of George's women, I suppose?' she said at last.

'You knew about them?' I asked before I could stop myself.

'I'd be a fool not to,' she said. 'They were his one great weakness. I paid no heed to them. George was aye careful. And he was not robbing me of anything. We were long past that sort of foolishness between ourselves.'

Mr Grogan phoned me later that week. I slipped away to visit him in Glasgow. He had discovered that the painting of the geese had been tacked over another canvas. The hidden oil-painting, which was a finished work except for the filling-in of some peripheral details, depicted what I can only describe as an orgy. Each of the ladies in his sketches made a fresh appearance while the men all sported military moustaches and were no longer in their first youth. The same exuberant joy and affection glowed from the canvas.

We agreed that Mr Grogan would mount the two pictures back to back, with the usual finish of brown paper to hide the less conventional work. The double picture still hangs in the sitting room. I have never looked at the hidden half again, but I like to know that it is there.

It would be pleasant to finish by reporting that the other characters all lived fairly happily for quite a long time, but life is not like that.

Bruce Fullerton was never charged with the murder of his first wife. But his weekend journey from New

York was tracked, the body was exhumed, an empty tin which had once held pistol powder was dug up in his garden and he was convicted, mainly on grisly scientific evidence, of the murder of the second Mrs Fullerton. The charge of murdering George Muir was found Not Proven. On the charge of attempting to murder Isobel, he was acquitted for lack of evidence.

Sergeant Bedale was congratulated in open court on the diligence of her investigation, but she never managed to live down the circumstances of the arrest. The story followed her around, growing all the time, during the remainder of her police career and the nicknames which attached to her were various but universally sexist. She stuck it out for a year and then retired to be a good wife and, later, a mother. This was what her husband had always wanted, so my thoughtlessness made at least one person happy.

3 2395 00316 4932